Rest From The Quest

Rest From The Quest

by
Elissa Lindsey McClain

HUNTINGTON HOUSE INC.
Shreveport, Louisiana

To the Baby Boom Generation (circa 1945-1964), now the largest segment of America's population, who led the spiritual quest in hopes of ushering in the New Age for the twenty-first century.

"If you want to know what it is like upon the path ahead, ask the ones who are leaving."

Unknown Saying

Acknowledgements

I shall always be grateful to my dear parents, Ray and Dorothy Lindsey, who instilled within me the desire to seek spiritual priorities in my quest for truth and who loved me through all the changes.

My love to my blessed husband, "Red," who diligently supported me and encouraged me to press on.

Introduction

In *The Hidden Dangers of the Rainbow*, I noted that the average New Ager's involvement in that Movement was innocent. I felt they wished to help, not harm people and that often they had been sucked in by appeals to their finest and best motives. Once there, they were held in the Movement by sophisticated forms of mind control.

Elissa McClain is not the typical New Ager. She did not become a New Ager, she was *raised* a New Ager. Reared in a Rosicrucian home, her first acquaintance with the Lord Jesus Christ was as an adult. This came through a reading of the Aquarian Gospel which presented a different Jesus — and a very different gospel. However, reading that book, Elissa became intrigued with this Jesus, distorted as his image was in that very book designed to lead Christians from Jesus — not New Agers to Him. From there, she read a *real* Bible and learned God's real truth!

Her story gives one a rare perspective on the emotions felt by one first trapped in the New Age Movement and then the frustrations felt upon leaving the Movement and encountering similar problems within the confines of Christianity.

Elissa's story contains important lessons for those dealing with New Agers. Tact and wisdom must be used. One leaving the New Age Movement often has "one eye in Paris and the other in Hong Kong." They have had their perceptions played with to a significant degree and it often takes a long time before they are completely healed. Books such as Elissa's *Rest From the Quest* and Johanna Michaelsen's *The Beautiful Side Of Evil* are important testimonies that can help both the recovering former New Ager see God's truth even more strongly and help the church understand the intense emotional struggles of those who have been caught up in the intricacies of the New Age Movement.

I must confess to having a "soft spot" in my heart for those who have renounced the New Age Movement. Often they have had both their economic and social life tied to it. Elissa did. It takes a great deal of courage to walk away from such inducements. Elissa, as have many others in the past three years, had the courage of her convictions and did leave the Movement, even though the cost was considerable. Elissa counted the cost and found what she was exchanging the New Age Movement for was more than adequate recompense.

Second Thessalonians 2:10 gave a profile of those who would be taken in by the deceptions of the Antichrist:

> *"And with all deceivableness of unrighteousness in them that perish; because they received not the love of the truth, that they might be saved."*

One must observe that this specified the *Love of the*

Truth — not necessarily those with "perfect truth." Elissa had the love of the truth, but she for many years did not have perfect truth. When confronted with God's truth, she fearlessly made the necessary changes in both her philosophy and life-style, and most importantly of all, she turned from occult initiations to trust and confidence in Jesus Christ.

Only when she rested from her long quest and in the Lord Jesus Christ did she find the peace she so fervently sought. I pray her candid story and observations will help thousands more find the true light of the world they are seeking and mistakenly think they have found within the New Age Movement. I further pray it will help Christians deal with New Agers in a spirit of empathy and love rather than rancor and spite. "They overcame the beast by the blood of the Lamb and the word of their testimony." May we do likewise.

Constance E. Cumbey

Table of Contents

Preface

There has been another Watergate. This time in religion.

The New Age Movement has been exposed. The results of a three-year investigation of the Movement's origins, methods, organizations and spokespersons has been documented in the book *The Hidden Dangers of the Rainbow* by Constance Cumbey, an attorney from Detroit, Michigan.

Information supporting Mrs. Cumbey's findings has been published in the book *Peace, Prosperity, and the Coming Holocaust,* by Dave Hunt, an internationally recognized expert on cults and world religions and a man who holds a Ph.D. in mathematics. His book includes a scenario of New Age tactics that should be required reading for both Christians and New Agers.

Both books contain alarming evidence that:

● Disciples of the Aquarian "masters" are preparing those on a spiritual quest to accept Lucifer as not one to be feared, but as a "master" who comes to restore man to wholeness, and that one wishing to enter the New Age must submit to a Luciferic initiation.

● Aryanism (purity of race or race-consciousness) threads through the teachings of Initiates of Wisdom from ancient legends of lost continents to current twenty-first century philosophies.

● New Age doctrines can be traced to Hindu religion, regardless of attempts to "westernize" the East-Indian belief in reincarnation, pluralistic gods and self-deification.

● New Age leaders who have been active politically are preparing people everywhere for a one world religion, a one world government and a world dictator.

● People of all religions who are looking for their messiahs are being conditioned to expect only one, Lord Maitreya, who will embrace all believers.

● The world "Plan" by New Age "Wise Persons" is practically identical to Adolph Hitler's SS Occult Bureau in Germany on which Nazism was founded.

● Orthodox Jews, Muslims and persons who acknowledge a personal relationship with Jesus Christ and who accept the authority of the Holy Bible are not welcome in the New Age Movement and are viewed as a threat to the "Plan."

● The "inner circle" of New Age leaders is fully aware that the religion they support is clearly that which the Bible describes as the religion of the Antichrist in the last days. However, the average New Age quester has been blissfully ignorant of the dangers in the rainbows they have been chasing.

Individuals all over the world have been reporting similar suspicions of a conspiracy — as have Constance Cumbey and Dave Hunt.

They include former Hindus, a career FBI man who once described himself as an agnostic and rock performer Kerry Livgren from the group *Kansas* who writes of his quest in *Seeds of Change*.

A radio announcer said he "cried like a baby" when he first heard Constance Cumbey confirm his own discoveries about the New Age Movement.

Through the years none of us fully grasped the magnitude of the influence of the New Age. But, based on what we did understand, we spoke out and faced criticism and mockery from those who refused to believe anything so diabolical could actually be taking place. We were suspected of irrational paranoia.

Somehow, while grieving about the severity of the issue, we confessed a relief that others like Constance Cumbey and Dave Hunt were more qualified and certainly more courageous than the rest of us to take a stand on God's promise in Daniel 11:32, ". . . *the people that do know their God shall be strong and do exploits.*"

I have listened to New Agers who have read the Cumbey and Hunt books. Some insist that the books left them unconvinced that they were vulnerable to any Aquarian Conspiracy.

Frankly, I find this incredible. Who would want *anything* to do with practices or beliefs where the ultimate spiritual goal is to accept an initiation to Lucifer?

To these die-hards I can only say, if you won't accept the warnings from a trial lawyer trained to examine evidence and if you won't listen to experts in world religions or heed the passionate pleas of concerned Christians that you turn around, would you consider the urgings from me — one who came up through the ranks of metaphysics and mysticism from childhood?

While I do not pretend to be an expert, I did spend the first twenty nine years of my life as a "street-level" New Ager, one who accepted the handed-down philosophies of "higher level" leaders in the "network" right from the beginning and for all those years.

1

A Psychic's Legacy

"Spooky Frank" was my great uncle. His railroad buddies called him that ever since the British immigrant woke up from a nap in the caboose and described a prophetic dream. Frank saw the train run through a farmer's cart loaded with white chickens, with feathers flying everywhere. When he opened his eyes and told the men about the accident, they laughed.

When the train pulled into the next town the fireman met up with Frank's crew and said that the engine had struck a cart full of chickens. "You should have been up front to see it! It was like snow!"

The crewmen looked at Frank and each other as though they'd seen a ghost.

Frank was accustomed to ghosts. Born in England among a family that believed in supernatural beings, psychic abilities and apparitions, he moved to America in his teens, bringing his beliefs with him. He married

one of my grandmother's sisters and remained childless.

Grandma had three young children when her husband
died and my mother, Dottie, was the oldest. It was hard
times for the widow and Grandma was grateful when her
sister and brother-in-law offered to take care of my
mother Dottie. She quickly became a live-in servant to
these well-to-do relatives. While she was still a little girl
she spent hours polishing their silver, waxing the spiral
staircase and washing dishes in the early morning before
school started.

But life in the big house was not all drudgery. Often
while mother sat quietly in the corner reading her books
Uncle Frank would lapse into a trance. He spoke in
different voices to bring messages from the unknown
realms.

At other times he conducted seances for people and
mother watched in amazement as tables floated and
spirits rapped out signals of their arrival.

Mother's favorite memory was the time a German
woman came to visit. The woman had studied music in
her homeland and talked about delicious German choco-
late treats. My great aunt discussed piano lessons while
Uncle Frank leaned back in his chair dozing. Then he
started to go into one of his trances.

"Ssh!" Aunt Bertha cautioned. "He has a message for
us — maybe just for you," she addressed her visitor.

In thick, guttural German, Frank spoke words to the
woman which made her shriek and fall on her knees
crying. She answered Frank in German. Everybody
knew that he didn't know the language; he was strictly a
"limey." But to my mother's amazement, the stranger
carried on a complete conversation with her uncle.

When Frank came out of his trance he didn't remember a thing. He had to be told that the spirit of a man, who had once been a candy shopkeeper in a German village, returned to pay the music teacher a visit.

Mother was convinced that none of the phenomena were tricks. She'd seen too many up close. How she loved her Uncle Frank. When he passed on to "the other side" the family hoped that he would contact them someday.

"Spooky Frank" didn't leave without successors. Mother carried his memory with her and his interest in psychic exploration would be perpetuated for generations in the family.

Relatives shuttled my mother back home but now it was to help support her brother and sister. Shortly afterward her brother joined the service and her sister ran off to get married.

But mother had better plans; she wanted to be a teacher. Yet she just couldn't shake the feeling of being a misfit everywhere she went. How long would it take before she felt her life really had meaning?

An early marriage and a quick divorce didn't help mother's self-esteem, either. She never did fulfill her desire to teach; instead she settled for a secretarial career.

At the age of thirty two, she made a decision to trust God for a husband. If she were supposed to remain single for the rest of her life, she'd need some kind of sign. If not, she was ready for marriage.

Four days after her prayer for a sign the most eligible man in the office — a man named Ray — asked her for a date. Silver-haired, distinguished and recently widowed, Ray had an attractive, homespun charm and seemed to radiate with a touch of mystery. No secretary would let this catch slip through her fingers!

Five years after their marriage, mother received startling news in a doctor's office. Instead of a bothersome tumor that could have been surgically removed at her earliest convenience, the results of the X-ray revealed quite a different diagnosis.

"Well, Dorothy, this is good news!" The doctor smiled and announced, "That's not a tumor after all; you're pregnant! About six months, I'd say."

It might have been good news to most childless women but for a career woman approaching her forties it only created worry and bewilderment.

Childbirth in general terrified her. Her own mother had nearly died in labor and at the time doctors weren't certain they could even save the baby. My mother and grandmother miraculously survived but religious differences among their relatives became an issue if a choice had to be made over which should be allowed to die! My mother didn't want to face a similar dilemma.

The reality of her pregnancy stirred other fears. Her age, her poor health and the fact that her husband, at fifty two, was already a grandfather from his previous marriage all contributed to the panic of giving birth. Abortion was too risky; there was only one solution: look for a doctor who would agree to performing a caesarean delivery.

At last she located an osteopathic surgeon and they scheduled the operation a month early "to avoid complications in case of miscalculation."

It was all so incredibly convenient. She was placed under sedation and remained unconscious throughout the operation.

I was born — with no heartbeat, no breathing. Nearly sixteen minutes ticked away before the frantic doctors administered a shot of adrenalin to my leg and at last I took my first breath. The injection that saved my life later developed into a small tumor which had to be surgically cut out, leaving a gaping hole in my thigh.

The details surrounding my existence were explained in esoteric terms. The doctor had told my mother that her baby's life began at the moment of the first breath and recorded the event "at 11:16 a.m." This became significant years later when discussions arose concerning the "Holy Breath of life" and determining exact times for astrological charts. If I had been born a month later I would have arrived under the Zodiac sign of Virgo, an "earth sign." Instead, I was a "Leo," associated with fire and its descriptions sounded so much more regal than the practical characteristics of the "Virgin." A bold and courageous lion seemed to have a more promising future.

Even the scar that marked my thigh was a mystical reminder that "God has important plans for you to have spared your life," my mother assured me. "You spent an awfully long time without oxygen when you were first born. Thank God you weren't handicapped severely."

When we chanced upon the information that, according to Greek philosophy, pregnant mothers were trained to look upon "things beautiful and serene" for positive effects upon the growing entity within them, mother worried that it might have been her fault that I developed a tumor. After all, she'd been preoccupied about tumors during her pregnancy.

"I honestly didn't know I was pregnant," she fretted. "If it hadn't been for the X-ray, I would *really* have been surprised. You didn't move at all until much later."

It seemed understood that "whatever you focus your attention upon, it shall come to pass." Mind over matter was a way of life.

Difficult births, we believed, were evidence of a soul's reluctance to return to earth. The physical plane was a testing ground for mankind and some of us had missions here to assist in the elevation of spiritual values and goals. It was up to the ones who were "cosmically aware" to encourage each other along the spiral of enlightenment, no matter how distressing life on earth appears to be. This wasn't the reality, anyway. It was only an illusion. Our task was to maintain a consciousness where sickness, poverty and disorder didn't exist.

I had no idea what my particular mission was going to be but there seemed to be constant clues. As an only child with older parents I had plenty of time for quiet reflections. Once when I complained to my mother that I wished I had smoother hands like other girls mother told me about a little old lady who visited us when I was a baby.

"She looked into your eyes for a long time and then she examined your palms. See all those lines?" Mother traced my hands affectionately. "The lady told me that you must be a very wise, old soul!"

Mother's comments contributed to my sense of self-worth and they seemed to assuade tendencies to be shy and withdrawn. I enjoyed the quietness of my parents' home and while they read books and listened to classical music I pondered about the mysteries of the universe.

My parents believed in reincarnation and I shared that belief. It was not unusual for me — when I was only five years old — to comment from the back seat of the car as we drove past a cemetery, "I wonder if I was a boy or a girl last time?" (My question became a vivid memory because it was the first time that I had a peculiar sensation of watching the surroundings from a faraway vantage point).

Obviously I shared my father's interest in metaphysical ideas and it looked as though I would make a good student of Rosicrucians. Daddy was a member of that secret organization and he knew about cosmic consciousness, ancient mystery religions and the Great White Brotherhood of planetary masters or avatars. He had even attained the learned art of psychic healing.

As soon as I could read I began studying "Lessons for Children in Rosicrucians," the series called "Torchbearers."

One story in particular described primeval cavemen sitting around their fire-altar. The gods had bestowed upon them a gift from the heavenlies which warmed them and gave light. The families of cavemen huddled around the flames and gnawed hungrily at the raw meat until they'd had their fill. Then the leader ceremoniously tossed a scrap of flesh into the fire as a sacrificial offering to the god of fire. The flesh sizzled and sent a tantalizing aroma drifting to the nostrils of the grateful cavemen.

One family member grumbled over the cold, wet meal of raw meat and he jealously savored the scent of sacrificial flesh roasting on the altar. When no one was looking he snatched the morsel for himself and triumphantly chewed his stolen prize.

It was good. Why should the gods have all of the best? Surely man was more intelligent than the beasts of the wilderness. Man is entitled. Cooked meat was invented!

The theory of evolution was threaded into these lessons but a more enlightened concept, that of spiritual evolution, permeated. In my metaphysical studies I learned that heavy meat was not only an unhealthy food product but that "animals die with a fear consciousness" and humans take on this vibration when they eat animal flesh. Abstaining from all meat and its by-products was a worthy goal, since meat-eating was considered grossly unspiritual. My father became the strictest of vegetarians some years later and I gave meat up for three and a half years during an intensified spiritual period later in my life.

Studying "Torchbearers" was interesting but I was impatient to get on with deeper things of God. After complaining to daddy that I really didn't want to sit down and go over these lessons, I was surprised that he didn't criticize me for my lack of discipline. He merely folded the booklets away and never mentioned them again.

Anyway, I was more fascinated with his practice of metaphysical healing.

Mother told me about times he had been able to alleviate all kinds of fevers and illnesses during my infancy and he performed the treatments from distant towns where he travelled on business. These were called "absent treatments" and often my father would retreat to his private bedroom (which mom affectionately dubbed his "Inner Sanctum"). Then he meditated upon names of friends or family members suffering from various ailments and within days we heard reports of their recoveries.

Daddy also knew another healing technique called "contact treatment." He prepared himself with deep breathing exercises and squeezed his thumb strategically before placing his hands on particular areas of my neck. Several times mother and I both gained benefits from these treatments. Migraine headaches, stubborn colds and even minor abrasions responded to his touch.

We couldn't know exactly how daddy did this because mom and I were not actual members of the Rosicrucians. We sat and whispered to each other while he secluded himself in his room filled with gadgets that hooked up to his stereo and tape recorder. These tools enabled him to program his subconscious with "sleep messages" on prosperity and health.

Mom said he'd also been experimenting with levitation of small objects and I sometimes heard him chanting low vowel sounds. We may have shared his interest but his privacy was very important to him so mom attended to her handicrafts and I read books.

I couldn't talk to anyone about our religious beliefs (since "some people are superstitious," I was informed) and I had few friends. I filled the void with an invisible companion named Johnny. He took the blame for the broken vase on the floor and I chatted with him for hours in my bedroom. Mom seemed amused instead of annoyed and she even humored me by including a place setting at the table for Johnny.

Shortly before we moved from Michigan to Florida my parents noticed that I hadn't mentioned my imaginary playmate for several weeks. I announced that he had moved away. They assured me that I'd make some *real* friends in my new home and, except for a brief encounter with an invisible horse, I ceased talking to playmates that only I could see.

When I was a child, Florida was like paradise to a nine-year-old, yet it contained its perils. I could go swimming in the ocean during the winter but I had to watch out for the burning stings of the Portuguese man-of-war. Exotic fruits were free for the picking but it was important to know which plants not to eat or certain death would follow. I loved to catch the little chameleons but other reptiles like coral snakes and rattlers shared the underbrush with scorpions. Even the bravest native Floridians seldom went barefoot in their own back yards.

Nevertheless, I took to the tropics immediately and loved to hear the rustling sounds of warm breezes through the palm fronds while wintering robins and cardinals settled on the lawn.

Next door was a family of seven children and I got acquainted with their oldest daughter Jan. We talked about God and where heaven really was. Jan, being a good Catholic girl, wanted to be a nun.

In an attempt to get me "churched," my mother took me to a Methodist Sunday school where boisterous youngsters sailed paper airplanes at the befuddled teacher.

The only Christian instruction I remembered was something about our souls being ruined by sin. The teacher picked up a felt-tipped marker and drew a black blot in the center of the paper. "This represents sin. Now, as you can see, the paper is no good anymore. It's the same way with your soul when it has sin in it."

At the church's confirmation ceremony I fidgeted with my ribbons and bows and ached to get into my shorts and T-shirt. An hour's worth of "Torchbearers" would have been more welcome than a stuffy ceremony. We were supposed to invite Jesus into our hearts and I accepted the ritual with as much enthusiasm as I did a measles inoculation.

The only time daddy joined us at this church was during holidays. He continued his metaphysical studies at home while mom begged him to attend for appearances as a family.

Then we found Unity.

Now here was a church where all three of us fit in. More than that, Unity became a springboard for my own personal Quest. The church logo, a winged globe, represented the goal of lifting up the consciousness of mankind with one unified religion for the world.

I didn't know I was about to discover some additional doctrines that promised amazing powers through the conditioning of the mind.

2

Unity and
Christ-Consciousness

We'd been invited to Unity School of Practical Christianity by Charlie, my mother's employer, who owned a pharmacy. Charlie mentioned that he'd been meeting with some other travellers on the Quest. They assembled in a rented building across from the drug store since their new building was still under construction. It was called "The Upper Room" and the minister was a woman.

We children had to meet in the Lion's Club, another building. What a perfect place for a little Leo! Mom and dad dropped me off and they hurried to their assembly. We all compared notes when we got home.

Sometimes I was the only fifth-grader in my class. Mom worried about my lack of companionship and suggested that I might be happier at a local Methodist church. She even considered enrolling me in a parochial school just for healthy discipline but I defended my new-found Unity and threatened to run away from home if I weren't allowed to continue with metaphysics.

After all, I was learning things that were expanding my outlook. I became more self-confident through "subconscious conditioning," and Unity's positive thinking doctrine pulled me out of my shell.

We did experiments with our minds and one student, Anna, successfully "willed" away an unattractive wart on her hand. We rejoiced with her for her abilities. However, it wasn't long afterward that we would share in her grief.

Anna's parents owned five horses and my friend was the envy of all horse-crazy girls. One Sunday Anna arrived at class and sobbed out the disaster that met her beloved pets.

"I can't believe it. They were all on the railroad track at the same time. They must have been running single file when the train just plowed through every one of them. Oh, how I'll miss Sheba; she was just a filly."

We hugged Anna but could not help her. We didn't know the metaphysical pattern that whenever something was gained something else was lost. Anna had been healed of warts but had lost her prized horses.

After comforting our friend we settled down to our class lesson and began to study on prosperity.

We were to design a poster board "Treasure Map."

"The center of the poster board should contain a picture that represents your concept of God," the teacher said. Some kids chose swirls of colors; others could only write in "God-Mind" or "Christ-Self."

The color of the board itself was also important: green for money or gold for true prosperity, pink for love; each was spiritually significant. We worked on our project for two weeks, cutting out pictures from catalogues of items we desired.

Very soon our "Treasure Map" paid off. Classmates reported that extra babysitting jobs came in, paper routes were offered and unexpected checks arrived. We were all excitedly experiencing thought-produced material blessings.

Meanwhile, the thrill of sharing metaphysics with church friends wasn't reflecting the troubles I was having with my neighborhood friends. I lived in a resort mobile home community where an unbalanced group of different ages made it difficult to make friends. The only girl my age was a rough-and-tumble tomboy who seemed to sway everyone to her whims. She didn't like me at all.

I wondered where all the neighborhood kids disappeared at five-thirty every day while I was completely excluded. I discovered the answer when some parents in the neighborhood called a special meeting to discuss a "secret hate club" their children had organized. I was shocked to discover that I was the object of their contempt. It seemed that I couldn't escape being viewed as "different," and I was miserably wounded.

In defense I became even more aloof. Classmates at school ignored me or taunted me for being stuck up but I refused to let anyone see me cry. I'd walk for blocks before giving into the lump in my throat and the sting in my eyes. When I was alone I sobbed quietly as I could so no one would hear me. Mother consoled me and cautioned against any retaliation toward my tormentors since it would only "bring you down to their level of negative emotions."

I was supposed to be above all that. I practiced forgiving my enemies and secretly felt much more mature than they.

It also gave me a great feeling of satisfaction to know that my family was the only one on the block that hadn't reacted out of fear when a history-making hurricane threatened our area. The entire neighborhood vacated to safer grounds, but we stoically remained.

"Fear is the opposite of faith," we affirmed. We prayed the Unity prayer of protection "Wherever God is, I am," and sat out the storm.

When the hurricane completely avoided our trailer park we learned that instead it had zeroed in on precisely the area where the "hate club" instigator had sought refuge with her family.

We felt blessed and triumphed over our application of "truth, not fact."

Although most Unity students didn't condemn one another for failing to achieve mastery over negative conditions, we knew that it was a daily struggle to "see only the good in every situation." The *facts* might be that we felt sick or were financially troubled, but the *truth* was that we were created to be healthy and prosperous. The object was to see life through the innocence of an Edenic state of mind and denying the negative helped us to affirm the positive. We expected to see our desired results through mental conditioning, no matter how contrary the appearances.

It was an inside joke to call these affirmations and denials "Unity lies." If somebody complained about being sick, another would prod, "There is no sickness, remember?" Then the aching student would retort, "Right. But this sure is a rotten illusion!"

We didn't acknowledge the existence of evil (that was only a misuse of good and since God was all that there was and God is good, no evil exists except in the minds of man) nor did we accept the reality of a devil (merely a

scapegoat for the unenlightened). We had no one to
blame but ourselves for our failures. New Thought religion presented the concepts of reincarnation, so cause
and effect was our responsibility.

While my Unity church remained as a sanctuary for
the enlightened members, its open-door policy for psychic exploration offered a method for me to make friends
at school. In the sixth and seventh grades in my free time
I began to study numerology and handwriting analysis
along with astrology. I quickly discovered that when I
could reveal something about others that no one else
could know I not only made my classmates *feel* important but it made me *look* important. Soon I was gaining
popularity at school and at church.

The Y.O.U. (Youth of Unity) voted me as an officer
and I qualified as a delegate to Unity Village Head-
quarters in the Kansas City area of Missouri. Four times
I visited the center where roses graced the plazas and
where vegetarian menus were standard. There was even
a tasty drink called a "metaphysical screwdriver."

These were the days before "What's your sign?" became an astrological cliche'. America's youth were still
dancing to surfer songs but we who felt like travellers in
the New Age agreed that we were light years ahead of our
own generation. Our peers were busy with fast cars,
beach parties and challenging the traditions of their
parents.

The rock song "Age of Aquarius" hadn't yet been
recorded but the youth of Unity chanted affirmations set
to music and sang about the spiritual evolution of mankind.

At the Village hundreds of delegates gathered for
group meditations and brain/mind lectures. Ministers
and authors shared their insights with eager teenagers

who took notes by day and at night sneaked off in pairs for more physical exchanges. We Florida girls were especially delighted that the California boys took to us so readily. Their reports of the enlightened West Coast magnetized our souls as powerfully as their worldly ways aroused our adolescent passions.

By the beginning of the next decade our beliefs were published by a California-based woman minister in her book *Seed For A New Age* (Doubleday & Co.). Sue Sikking, with teenagers of her own, presented us with an updated handbook which suggested that people take the '60s generation seriously.

On the book's cover two rainbows decorated the title. The arc beneath was inverted.

A few choice "seeds" include:

"Man, you are your assignment. Man is going to redeem himself."

"So many signs for the times are called evil but they are man learning the lesson of his God-Self. This is the preparation for the advancement of mankind."

"The (New Birth) is the transformation that is taking place in us that we interpret as evil or something that can hurt us."

"Where does all the seeming adverse power originate? All other power is but a fragment of this one Power."

"The propaganda that our world is a fallen one. . . is a delusion."

"When we believe in predestination. . . we commit the great sin of submission."

"To be separated is sin, but in reality, there is no separation."

"The great instructions from within come through the soul to the human mind in times of meditation when it becomes a silent waiting instead of active thought."

"Pure fantasy is the highest dream . . . LET'S DREAM!"

"We may approach our God in different ways but in whatever way we feel comfortable."

"Many times divorce is the result of outgrowing each other in interests and in consciousness. We unfold at different rates and come to spiritual maturity at different times."

"Oneness with others can be found only within ourselves. If you find soul satisfaction and a soul mate, you have completed something within yourself."

"Prove your Sonship!"

"We are in the process of finding the world transforming vitality and enthusiasm of God. We are searching for the seed of the New Age. Now is the time. We are the people!"

The teenagers at Unity didn't have to wait until the seventies to confirm that "we are the people" of the New Age. There was no generation gap, either, for whenever we met older individuals who shared our cosmic dreams we had instant gurus.

One of our favorites was Crystal. She told us how she saw people's auras and we stood in line for readings of our color-energy. Crystal communicated with nature spirits and we glowed warmly when she said, "All of us are special to God. It's just that some of us know it."

Crystal became my mentor and I patterned myself in her image. She was an artist and her flamboyant appearance was a delight to young and old. Before the time of my high-school graduation it was evident that I would have to decide upon a career. Crystal was a major influence in the path I selected.

The Unity church, now an impressive expanse of hexagons and corridors, added a preschool unit. Occasionally I assisted with the toddlers during church hours and our minister offered me a teaching scholarship.

"If I could intern under Crystal, perhaps I could grow spiritually at the same time I was learning to be a teacher," I commented to my mother. She was pleased that I might consider a career that she'd shelved years ago.

Teaching did, after all, provide a more practical means of independence than the vocation suggested by my guidance counselor.

Since I didn't have the mechanical skills for business that my mother had acquired and I knew that the college funds my parents had set aside were depleted when dad was hospitalized for pancreatitis, I was thrilled when the counselor told me the results of her review.

"You seem to do well in the areas of speech, journalism and creative writing. Most of your articles show that you are interested in inspirational slants," she observed. "We have a work/study program for the students. Instead of attempting to be a secretary or a salesperson, perhaps you'd be interested in writing."

The thought of writing articles for Unity magazines and the Village Publishing Company in Missouri was exhilarating.

The counselor shuffled some papers and continued, "Of course you will have to take the entrance exam for the program. After that, I'll see what I can arrange."

For the next two weeks I tried to choose between being a teacher of metaphysics with Crystal or sharing views with other celebrated authors from Unity like James Dillet Freeman, the poet. One of his poems, "I Am There" accompanied America's first astronauts. Freeman had once autographed my copy of his poems at a Unity youth conference and he became a staff writer for Unity periodicals.

In one booklet simply called "Unity" the writer described his communication with the prophet Jesus during meditation. Freeman quoted the conversation Jesus revealed to him concerning an exchange between the adolescent Galilean and a friend. Young Jesus had become upset about the sacrifices of lambs and doves in the temples and lamented to his companion about the injustices of these rituals:

"I don't believe in a God who would demand a sacrifice of someone's son, and neither do you . . . I don't think God wants us to bow down before him in fear and trembling. I think that's what's wrong with things now. There is too much fear in the world. Fear only gives rise to more fear. . . I don't want to question the wisdom of the priests and scribes, I just want to find a little wisdom for myself."

Apparently the message from Jesus explained an event from "the missing years" of Christ. I hadn't heard any messages from Jesus but I knew I was at a crossroads in my life. I prayed that God would let me know which direction I should take and nervously anticipated the entrance test. I decided that if I couldn't pass the test I'd know enough to enroll as a kindergarten teacher.

To my surprise I passed the exam above several other hopefuls. During my next appointment with the guidance counselor I received wonderful news.

"You can take your classes in the morning and then in the afternoon you can study under a famous author who lives right here in Boynton Beach," she was saying. "Have you ever heard of Catherine Marshall? She also writes inspirational articles."

The name was familiar but I hadn't read anything by the woman. That didn't matter. I was going to be a writer!

That aspiration fizzled when my mother reminded me that I wanted my own car and an apartment after graduation and "writers don't make much money."

"You're only seventeen," mom pointed out. "What could you write about at your young age? You've hardly had any real life experiences."

Mom was right. My heart sank. I declined the counselor's arrangement and never did meet Mrs. Marshall.

When our minister described the responsibilities of becoming a lead teacher in a private school and confirmed that Crystal would be my directress, I accepted the scholarship.

Two weeks after high school graduation I was sitting in a classroom taking endless notes from a European instructor. Professor Elisabeth Caspari had studied the teaching method under the founder Maria Montessori

when both were stranded in India during political tur-
moil. It was my fortune to learn Montessori training from
one of the pioneers of the system in America.

Crystal gave me a little book of Oriental philosophy
and, between compiling my notes as an intern, I continued exploring the path of eastern religions.

Our church was a center for several New Thought
activities. Some of the women who attended Unity were
more interested in Oriental flower arranging or Hatha
yoga for exercise. However, I preferred the dream semi-
nars and "inner circle" meetings where cosmic books
were circulating.

One of the women in my class furtively asked if I'd ever
tried LSD. She was older than I and owned a drive-in
restaurant. I knew it well; it was a favorite hangout for
teenagers. It seemed odd that this woman should ask me
if I knew where to get the hallucinogen. As far as I knew it
was still an experimental substance.

"I've read that it really expands one's consciousness,"
she whispered. "If you hear of any around, let me
know."

I nodded mechanically and avoided her during class
breaks. It didn't seem likely that I'd ever run into any
"contacts." Still, the idea intrigued me.

Was it really possible to "see God" like the reports
said?

3

Short Cuts to Nirvana

"During this seminar you will record every dream you can remember upon waking up," the visiting minister announced. "Have a notebook handy by your bed and practice telling your subconscious mind to wake you with the memory of your dreams intact. Anything significant — symbols, people, ideas, whatever you remember — you must include in your dream journal."

Some participants complained that they didn't dream very often, or at least it was difficult to remember. As usual, I knew this would be a snap. I dreamed every night and in color. My journal would be full.

In 1967 I had "the soul mate vision." I recorded it faithfully and the details of this dream had a powerful effect upon my relationships throughout the years.

Three men were represented in the dream, the first being dressed extravagantly in kingly robes and offering a ring of gold. The second was crude and shaggy and

presented a ring of silver. Next I found myself alone in a
misty garden gazebo, sobbing over having been aban-
doned by the first two men. Out of the shadows stepped
a fair-haired youth who only offered his hand to comfort
me, saying, "I am the one."

The clues were mysterious and it would take over ten
years to put all the pieces together, but I was certain of
one thing: I had glimpsed my true soul mate.

When two Jewish women who were enrolled in the
Montessori training class confirmed one of these clues,
they told me that some answers were contained in my
hands.

"See, here they are," the older woman turned over my
hands and traced my palms. "You'll be married twice,
and then you will find your real partnership."

I groaned at the thought of going through two marriages before attaining happiness. Ethereal dreams and
palm-reading made me impatient to know more. Several
women were meeting at the church to discuss a rumor
that a New Age center was being developed somewhere
in the mid-west. The group was studying a book called
The Ultimate Frontier by Eklal Kueshana and everybody was doing anagrams trying to figure out who the
author really was. "A community near Chicago" was the
only hint of the center's location but I purchased a copy
for myself and followed along.

This book mentioned the Great White Brotherhood,
Atlantis, Lemuria (the legendary submerged continents
of both coasts), and its writer expressed open contempt
for fundamentalist Christian religion. Some of the concepts were a bit extreme for the loving and non-judg-
mental adherents to Unity doctrine, but much of its
content was compatible.

Traditional churches who preach that "Jesus Saves"

were called "... traps for fools ... to attract membership
of the sinner who doesn't want to earn his salvation but
feels more comfortable believing that mere faith in
Christ will snatch him from the clutches of devils ...
(People) expect God to fill their needs without practical
compensation, but they childishly seek a mystic mumbo-
jumbo which will give them salvation without earning it.
They look for spiritual enlightenment ... as an outright
gift from a Holy Christ."

"There is no such thing as the Devil or a fallen angel
leading the forces of evil. Man alone is responsible for
the present discord in the world ..."

"Karmic indebtedness ... is another way of saying
unatoned sins."

"Christ took away the sins of the nations of the world
but not of any individual."

"Because the great angel Lucifer had been responsible for the abolishment of Eden in order that men could
begin on the road to spiritual advancement, the Katholis"
(a name given to the Lemurian priests who believed that
"their God would provide everything for the believer in
return for his true worship") "were led to believe that
this Angel was the most loathsome Ego ever associated
with the Earth."

"The truly happy Egos ... see only the good ..."

More details of the Great White Brotherhood were
revealed but, according to this account, the Brotherhood is not easily entered. It takes "three thousand
incarnations to become a Brother" and "each man must
elevate himself. No man can do it for him!" A great many
historical personages were spokesmen developed by the
Brotherhoods. For instance: "Moses and Socrates were
trained by the Hermetic Brotherhoods; Jesus and John

the Baptist and their respective parents by the Essene
Brotherhood; Buddha by the Brahmic Brotherhood;
and George Washington and Benjamin Franklin by the
Luciferian Brotherhood."

Three organizations are listed among the mundane
schools which "were nearing completion of the require-
ments" for the Luciferian school but apparently they
didn't live up to the Great White hopes, and "suffered
acutely from the general downgrading of student caliber":
Masonic Inner Court, Rosicrucian and Theosophist.

Nowhere in this book did I locate a single reference to
Jesus being followed by Christ. Each name was listed
separately but that wasn't unusual. We Unity students
knew that Jesus was a given name and Christ was an
acquired title, like *President*. Since we already had "the
Christ within," we had an inner mastery over conditions
and consciousness.

Just as my spiritual knowledge was growing, so was
my social world expanding. My generation had grown
right into an era tagged "the New Morality" and it was a
relief to belong to a church that wasn't hung up on myths
like sin or hell. (We only acknowledged two sins — if you
hurt someone intentionally or unintentionally). I had
become quite accustomed to having my own apartment
and one night it was the setting for quite a different
activity.

My Unity buddy Erick said he was coming over with a
tab of mescaline. It wasn't exactly LSD but better because it was a natural substance, like the peyote mushrooms that Mexican mystics used for their religious
ceremonies.

"I already dropped mine before I got here, so hurry
up," he said handing me the speckled tablet. (I thought

he meant he'd lost it somewhere but soon my awareness of street slang improved; he's already "swallowed" his portion).

I washed it down with water and waited. Erick waited. Nothing happened.

"Wow, you must have a weird metabolism," he observed. "You should have gotten off on this long before now."

I had a terrible urge to cry and I didn't know why.

"Erick, would you bring me a pillow from my room please." He obediently retrieved a cushion. I hung on to it, crying muffled sobs from the depths of my soul. It wasn't exactly the reaction Erick had hoped for or expected.

I mopped my face and apologized for being such a baby and ending up as a disappointing novice. Then the carpet began to swirl like a green ocean and I braced myself.

"Erick, I think I feel something."

"All right! Finally!" Erick made me stand up while he examined my eyes. "They're big as cat eyes! Look for yourself."

Making my way to a mirror I lost my equilibrium and grabbed for the wall. It felt as though my arm passed right through it and I nearly fell down.

"This is crazy." I stared at the room and watched patterns sway and turn.

"You know something," Erick said with a profound look on his face, "I really think it was because you were resisting the effects at first that it took so long. When you cried, it all sort of broke loose. Come on, I brought an album for you to listen to."

The directions on the record sleeve read, "To be played in the dark." Erick lit some candles and we

listened to musical renditions of each sign of the Zodiac.
"Leo" was bright and bouncy; "Pisces," which was
Erick's sign, was hauntingly melodic and ended with low
tones of chiming bells. Our favorite was the sign of
Aquarius, the water-bearer, symbol of brotherhood of
man.

Minutes seemed like hours. I wondered how I would
explain my condition to Cheryl, my roommate. She was
due to get off work soon and the chemicals in my system
kept me awake and wide-eyed. I asked Erick to leave and
waited for Cheryl to come home. When she opened the
door, I was still sitting in the dark pondering the sensations I was experiencing.

"What's the matter with *you*?" Cheryl asked casually.
"Got the blues?" She tossed the keys on the coffee table
and headed for the bedroom.

I sighed gratefully that she didn't question me further.
Cheryl was never interested in my metaphysical religion
and certainly she wouldn't approve of my psychedelic
"trip." Forcing myself to lie on my bed, I stared at the
ceiling and marveled that hours ago I had openly cried
in front of another human being. There was a ringing in
my ears, or was it a distant cathedral bell somewhere?

"Cheryl," I called out timidly. "Is there a church
nearby? I hear bells."

"Now I *know* you've flipped out. You're not only
mixed up with some religion that sounds like a Commie
plot, now you're hearing bells! Go to sleep, will you?"

Turning to the wall, I clamped my eyes shut. Why was
it that so many people were suspicious of spiritual inno-
vations? I needed someone to share the religious possibilities with me, someone like Erick from my own church.
The night sounds seemed louder than usual and it was
dawn before I could sleep. I hadn't seen God or wanted

to jump off any two-story buildings during my first trip on hallucinogens. Maybe there wasn't much wrong with these methods of mental perceptions. I hoped I'd at least marry somebody who was as "aware" as I.

For the next two years I filled my days with teaching school and my nights with youth group activities. I was a director for our chapter and I opened my apartment for the meetings. Only a handful of teenagers attended when we held our meetings at the church on Sunday mornings. But once the kids found out that I was letting them choose their own topics for discussions and that they could go surfing on Sunday mornings, the attendance swelled. The minister didn't seem to mind that the youth group had classes on week nights. When we had to meet twice a week because there were so many showing up that one meeting a week was not enough, the church was all too pleased.

The most popular topics were reincarnation, past-lives, psychic phenomena, and, of course, dating. I was too cautious to take any responsibility for teaching sexual morality so I left those topics alone. There wouldn't have been much time for that anyway since these were serious Questers who took sexuality in stride with their spiritual adventures.

These kids called themselves "C.A.T.S." (College Age Truth Seekers). They seemed to respect my insights and often they followed me to the Unity retreats and rallies (mini-conferences like at the Village) where Erick and I sang and played guitars. During one rendition of a song about the "mandala" (Hindu symbol of the karmic wheel of birth) an entire audience of college students gave us a standing ovation and screamed for more. Clearly my generation was catching up with the ideals of the Aquarian Age. Perhaps I'd find my soul mate after all.

I met a restaurant owner named Mark who was a Christian Scientist. He knew all about mind over matter and he told me about an uncle who treated a broken arm just by mental concentration. I was especially intrigued with the possibilities of communicating with Mark during his unconscious state. While napping he had carried on a complete conversation with me that lasted for nearly an hour yet when he awoke he had no memory of our communication. I considered marriage. However, Mark had one serious flaw. He was incredibly jealous. I backed out of the wedding plans and hoped that a near miss might be counted as one of my ill-fated marriages.

When I finally did consent to marriage it was with a flashy-dressed ambitious goal-setter. It seemed that our union would please our parents but we didn't share religious views. Out of marital boredom I practiced kundalini yoga in an attempt to raise the "creative life energy" that was supposedly hidden at the base of the spine. (My new husband wasn't into yoga).

"Kundalini" is a Hindu term for "coiled serpent" and the purpose of yoga, or "yoking," is to prepare the body and mind for meditation. Simple yoga, called "Hatha," is the most common among Americans and is the gentle exercises in the meditative process. As I practiced the deeper levels of yoga, the "coiled serpent" that I had unleashed presented me with a shocking surprise. I experienced a bluish-white flash of lightning in my brain and it scared me right out of going any further with that kind of yoga. The gentle exercises seemed safer.

It was 1970, and during the next two years I attended the play "Hair," sang along with the theme song "Age of Aquarius" and saw the movie Woodstock. I also saw the demise of my first marriage. It seemed like a good time to set out on my own and I decided upon Orlando, Florida. I'd heard that a Montessori administrator had several schools in that area and the owner of the schools had trained at my Unity church. I packed my belongings and headed upstate.

4

Chasing Rainbows

My teaching credentials had preceded me and I was accepted for a lead position in an Orlando school. I had learned much at Unity but now I was ready for additional advancement. When a minister of a Religious Science church whispered that his congregation considered Unity as a "spiritual kindergarten" I was certain that I would discover even deeper truths there.

This church was far more intellectually oriented and, instead of the cozy meditations, we practiced metaphysical methods in terms of brain-mechanics. The mind was divided into three parts: conscious, subconscious and super-conscious, just as Unity had taught. But there seemed to be less emphasis on the mystical and more on man's abilities. At Unity we had said in unison, "God is, I am." In Religious Science we invited Jewish scholars to speak on humanistic values and the necessity of mental discipline. Healing and prosperity were the major topics being discussed and I took pages of notes as if I were attending a college lecture.

One of the members was a mature, handsome man named Rudy. He had an "open marriage" where either partner was free to become involved with other people and jealousy was carefully avoided. Rudy's home became a mecca for dissatisfied couples who were seeking independence, and often marriages that had lasted several years fell apart as new "soul mates" took the place of long-term spouses. Rudy introduced his companions to bisexual encounters and all kinds of liaisons developed.

It was easy to understand bisexuality and homosexuality. After all, it was generally accepted that past-life carry-overs explained the tendencies for certain individuals to explore relationships with their own genders. Two of my high school friends had confided to me that they were gay and I was one of the few people who readily accepted them just as they were.

My own apartment hosted assortments of friends who discussed their lifestyles while smoking marijuana. One of our favorite party albums was a record about the effects of grass and we snickered at the familiar descriptions. On the cut called "Meditation" we listened to a satire of an East-Indian guru teaching his disciples to empty their minds and chant a mantra, or "meaningless sound" in preparation for tapping into the astral realms. As the mantra-chants grow louder the guru yells above the crowd "and we will rise above the physical realm, until we are all one!" Then the guru's Indian accent changes dramatically and sounds very German as he screams, *"Und soon ve vill take over ze vorld, und ve vill say it together. . ."* The voices thunder in a crescendo of *"Zeig Heil! Zeig Heil!"*

Anyone who had not previously heard the record would

shudder with icy chills and the rest of us would laugh at
the intended joke of paranoia that marijuana creates.

Some of my friends had turned to grass simply for
recreation but as their fascination for harder drugs in-
creased so did my yearning to find my soul mate.

When I met Rich I was attracted to his long hair and
his addictive charm. Before I could even rationalize that
I was really moving to Wisconsin with a man I hardly
knew, I told my parents that I was getting married again.
The wedding was attended by several gay friends of
mine and I wrote my own conditional vows. This marriage would really be the one that would last. I'd make
certain of that.

We had a shaky start. The day that the movers were
scheduled to pick up my furniture I was robbed of my
most precious possessions. And the policeman who came
to make out the report tried to molest me and was only
interrupted when the moving man arrived. On top of
everything else I learned that it had been a close friend
who had set up the robbery and I was beginning to think
that it was all a bad omen.

"Once again, something gained, something lost," I
cried pitifully. My new husband assured me that he'd
take good care of me and that we would return to Florida
as soon as he saved enough money from his job in Wisconsin.

Milwaukee was the Big City in my eyes. New Age
meetings were advertised in underground papers and
meetings for feminists with spiritual aspirations were
held frequently for consciousness-raising.

I was even hired by an administrator of a Montessori
school which rented from a Unity church and although
the school and church were not affiliated, the staff welcomed my viewpoints. Between 1973 and 1976 our little

school had a waiting list of parents who wanted their children to be part of our program. We did yoga with the children, insisted upon health food snacks and turned the traditional Montessori "thinking chair" (a disciplinary seat for reflection of behavior) into a meditation center complete with incense and a candle.

Rich introduced me to all kinds of hallucinogens that helped us to communicate with each other. Through drug-induced euphoria we felt an inter-connectedness with our companions and with all of nature. But we were always disappointed that the effects didn't last and we ended up seeing each other as "us and them."

A Unity friend invited me to attend a grand opening for the "Himalayan Institute for Biofeedback and Psychical Research" in Chicago. I hoped I'd find out more about the New Age community I'd read about in the book *Ultimate Frontier.*

Instead we met Swami Rama, the residing guru at the Institute. A robust man whose physique belied his age, the Swami boasted to his disciples that he could make cancerous lesions appear and disappear from his arm at command. We were treated to a machine that registered stress and trained the user to achieve the meditative alpha level of concentration. (That alpha level, also called astral realm, could also be reached through marijuana. Street people already knew that).

If a course in biofeedback wasn't actually mandatory for attaining the alpha level, neither was it necessary to become an official member of N.O.W. (National Organization for Women) to be part of the feminist movement. Ideals for liberation filtered down through the cosmic network and some leaders readily welcomed the New Age brand of spirituality. I attended consciousness-raising groups that went beyond the vicious criticism of men in general; it was understood that woman is a more spiritual being because of her psychic intuition.

Myths and legends always glorified the dominance of woman as high priestess and her affinity to the elements of nature was personified in the moon. Each of us was expected to balance both sides of our sexuality so both genders could cultivate masculine and feminine qualities. If a woman didn't find reciprocity with a man, we were encouraged to turn to each other for our religious needs.

Another mystery was that a soul *mate* wasn't even the ultimate companion. There was supposed to be a soul *twin* for each of us, another being who more closely mirrored the inner self. This soul twin might be a member of one's own family or of the same sex. It might even exist on another plane of reality. If an individual discovered that the soul twin was residing in a different realm, then meditation was the only way to astrally connect. The final union could only take place after transition. Hopefully, there was no need to submit to voluntary suicide to end the loneliness but it was always an option.

The depression of my own loneliness didn't warrant suicide but my relationship with my second husband grew stormy and cold. The only brightness in my days was the faces of the little children in the classroom. Jody, a new teacher, was hired as my co-directress and immediately we felt linked to one another.

A doe-eyed, statuesque brunette, Jody first visited me at my inner-city flat so we could discuss teaching style. She was carrying a vegetarian sandwich and offered me half. I was pleased to accept it.

"I've been practicing vegetarianism lately myself," I smiled. "Maybe you can give me a few recipes."

"Where I live there's lots of room to plant vegetables," Jody said softly. "I live in a cottage by a lake but we don't have any running water. Maybe you could come out and look around."

"I'd like that, thank you." I looked intently at Jody. She was so different from me, so quiet and introspective.

We arranged to scout the woods near her home. Jody showed me the odd puffball mushrooms that grew alongside the garden and as we walked in silence I was captured by her atunement with nature. She would be a steadying influence for me, I thought. I needed some peace and tranquility amidst the fast-lane of city life where Rich seemed to thrive. It would be a good teaching year.

That winter I "opened" my marriage. Jody's boyfriend was busy with his own liaisons and compassion was a rare commodity in my own home, too. It seemed very natural to explore the possibilities of intimacy with someone so sensitive as Jody, and Rich was baffled when I no longer badgered him for attention. I'd found a real soul sister.

Together Jody and I sought further clues to our existence at the home of an elderly Scottish woman who could "see" past lives and future events. She insisted that she was the mother of Jesus and also had been his mother in other lives. The old woman showed us books she claimed she'd written telepathically and recommended a few others with titles like *The Third Eye* and *The Aquarian Gospel*. She had portraits of several masters and yogis on a mantle in her sitting room. It seemed no one was left out of her collection.

I looked at the faces on the mantle and wondered if someday the old woman would be represented in the homes of seekers. She seemed so wise and mysterious. Jody had several of the same pictures in her meditation room but her favorite was Yogananda. According to the reports, the yogi's body had taken several days to decompose after his death — he was that advanced.

Our *menage a toi* might have reflected the casual arrangements that flourished in the seventies or the "Me" decade. But none of us counted on the side-effects. Somehow I was still restless and unsatisfied and one night I called an abrupt end to our trio. There were too many hurt emotions and not even a soul twin could fill the emptiness in my soul. Jody went back to her boyfriend, Rich spent more time at the bars and I kept praying that things would miraculously get better.

It *was* a miracle that at least my friendship with Jody wasn't severed. She invited me to assist with her boyfriend's new business in Kirlian photography and we experimented with different objects to compare the changes in auras. We set up their geodesic dome for the "aura-booth" at a science fair and called to passersby, "Come see the colors of your life-force!"

Curious takers watched as we placed their hands in a sleeve connected to a Polaroid camera. The customers were asked to try and relax more and more until they achieved a meditative state and then we showed them how the colors changed each time they moved their hands to another spot on the film. Little rainbows surrounded the fingerprints and even the skeptics acted impressed.

Our best-selling item was the large print of a marijuana leaf. Flares of reddish-gold light emanated from the famous trademark of pot-smokers. We all hoped that the Kirlian photography business would prosper as well as provide an open channel to enlighten others on the

Quest.

The Milwaukee Unity Questers were my colleagues at the school. One couple had been studying the teachings of Edgar Cayce, "America's Sleeping Prophet" as he had been tagged.

Cayce had been a Sunday school teacher but whenever he went into a trance his messages often disputed the Bible. His readings are still sought at his Virginia Beach institute and I asked the couple to locate Cayce's reference that one day Nebraska would be a coastal state. We didn't have any luck finding the quote but I wanted to confirm the general belief we New Agers held that Earth was scheduled for another flood. I had some relatives who lived treacherously close to the sites of the coming deluge and Atlantis was sure to rise again.

One of those relatives was a cousin of mine named Jaye who had shared my beliefs and when I last heard of her she was considering joining the Rosicrucians. She sent me a tape and I eagerly awaited the news of her latest discoveries. The contents of the tape were completely unexpected.

Jaye and her husband had renounced mysticism, esoterics, astrology, the works. They were now attending a Baptist church and saying something about a family member being attacked by demons! I couldn't believe what I was hearing! Jaye had been so enlightened. How could she chuck it all for backwards Christianity? It was more than I could comprehend. Well, maybe Jaye's father-in-law, my mother's brother, had convinced them that to keep peace in the family they'd all have to be Baptists. I shook my head and tried to think of a polite way to answer the tape.

Meanwhile I found an old Ouija board that one of my gay friends had given me years ago. There was little doubt that advanced seekers disdained such a juvenile game for the purpose of searching for wisdom but it was something to do. My sister-in-law Debbie agreed to work the board with me and we asked simple questions like who we were in previous lives.

The pointer flew rapidly as if impatient to get our answers out of the way and to get on to other more important messages. I was told I had lived in Great Britain and my name had been Elizabeth. When we asked where Debbie had lived prior to this incarnation, the board said "Venus." The idea that someone could have been on another planet intrigued us and, since my friend is truly a beauty, it was easy to see the connection to a symbol of love.

"Venus sounds great but how about a lifetime a little closer to home," I suggested. The board first said that Debbie had lived as Sarah in Jerusalem but then it spelled out that Debbie was a "witch." Both of us shuddered. Immediately I commanded the board not to speak such things of darkness. The board responded, "good witch." Somehow that news comforted us but I was curious to know just who or what was controlling this mystical parlor game.

"Identify yourself," I commanded. The "spirit guide" complied and the words formed:

"Saint Germain."

Long ago I had heard that name, somewhere in an organization that spoke of Mark Age or Golden Age. Someone named Astara spoke of St. Germain. I groped for clarity.

"Remind me to look that up sometime," I said to Debbie. We folded the board and never brought it up again.

Whenever I think of Debbie, I am reminded of a

tropical flower, the gardenia. It is exquisitely lovely and fragrant but bruises easily. Like the gardenia, my fragile friend was nearly crushed by possessiveness.

Debbie's marriage came to a merciful end after her husband repeatedly abused her and threatened suicide. His alcoholic binges were more than she could endure and she suffered an emotional breakdown. A holistic doctor tried to treat her for leukemia and it turned out she was just mildly anemic. My own marriage was following the same pattern and after continuous physical and mental torment I knew I had to get out of Milwaukee if I was going to survive at all. I said goodbye to Debbie, to Jody and to the best-paying job I'd ever had. All I could say to Rich was that I hoped someday he'd come to his senses and come back to me.

Instead, he made sure I couldn't afford to retrieve my belongings. He confiscated my car and refused to take me to the airport. So Jody took me. She softly expressed her sympathy that it was a shame I was leaving Wisconsin with only a guitar, a bike and a few personal items. When she put me on the plane Jody handed me two roses.

"The red one is for the person you have been," she said tearfully. "The white one is for the person you will become."

I hugged her gratefully and boarded the plane alone. Looking out the window I hardly felt like I was about to become anything but more miserable. I grabbed tightly to the rose bouquet in my hands and didn't even seem to feel the thorns digging into my palms. By the time I arrived in Daytona Beach the red bloom wilted and the white bud was beginning to open.

5

Terminal Karma

A blast of tropical wind swept my hair out of my eyes as I arrived in Daytona Beach. Quickly wiping the tears from my face, I forced a smile for my dear friend Sally. We had known each other since high school and shared our first apartment nearly a decade before. Sally was newly divorced and it looked as though we would again be roommates. I was immensely grateful to have a roof over my head.

Sally took my hand and said, apologetically, "I know you're probably depressed but there's a party going on in the apartment clubhouse. Do you think you're up to it?"

"Hey, when did you ever know me to turn down a party?"

I flippantly slung my over-sized bag across my shoulder and made my way to her car. I glanced at the passing buildings and hoped that I wouldn't have too far to ride a bike to my new teaching job.

"I think you'll like my friends," Sally was saying. "The girls are all divorced, too, and they'll show you around to the best discos. Wait 'till you meet my boyfriend. He's a golf pro!"

Wonderful, I thought. Sally was never interested in my cosmic beliefs and now I'd have to socialize with golf pros and disco dolls. The whole apartment-complex singles scene looked like tapioca compared to the bitter-sweet confections I'd tasted in the counter-culture. With my jeans and New Age accessories — feathers, rainbows and Mexican linens — I became the resident hippie.

I'd show these *girls* how we party in the city. Every Wednesday, Friday and Saturday night Sally's crowd met at a local dance bar where they sat scrutinizing male candidates for "Mr. Right." What little money I had I used with calculation. If a man bought me a drink, I'd buy him one back.

"There, now I don't owe you anything," I snapped. The rest of the women acted embarrassed to be seen with me; I was really sounding hard and tough. My jaded personality even surprised me.

The job that had been promised to me fell through when it turned out there were more teachers than en-rolled students. Without a car I couldn't be depended upon at a regular job. I offered to clean Sally's house and look after her boy in exchange for a bunk bed and a meal. My parents supplemented our collective income and I felt totally worthless — I'd be thirty soon and was still taking handouts from my folks.

Sally was talking about getting married again and I knew it was time for me to move on.

Back in Orlando, Gerry and Teresa, a married couple, took me in. They had known me for years and offered to pay me as a live-in babysitter. On my nights off I stayed out late, causing them deep concern for my welfare. I couldn't blame them for worrying. Some of my acquaintances didn't exactly fit in with their professional circles. I was more comfortable with other vagabonds who struggled with the inconsistencies of spiritual advancement and emotional stability.

In an attempt to explain these social outcasts to Gerry and Teresa I talked about karma and humility. Gerry wasn't impressed.

"Frankly, I've never believed all of that," he said flatly.

I thanked him for being so honest and shifted my conversation to learning more about what he and his wife *did* believe. They were more interested in psychology, humanism and studies about left-brain/right-brain.

Often I had the feeling we were talking about the same things but just used different jargon.

One afternoon while I was babysitting their toddler I picked up one of their psychology magazines. An article described a group of people out west who sold all their belongings and waited atop a mesa for UFOs to carry them away.

My eyes were getting heavy. The little boy was napping quietly in his room and I allowed myself to drift into sleep. Suddenly I heard a loud buzzing in my ears and I was conscious of being drawn up out of my body. For a moment I thought I was being "beamed aboard" some hovering aircraft. My heart pounded wildly. As the sensation intensified I remembered the sleeping child and my responsibility. Immediately I snapped back to my physical body.

If I were going to go on any cosmic space flight it would have to be another time.

The experience obsessed me and after it occurred repeatedly I looked for more information to explain it. Apparently I wasn't being transported by friendly aliens; I was merely experiencing involuntary astral projection. One of the signals was a whirring sound. I tried to practice "O.O.B.E.s" (Out Of Body Experiences) but couldn't get farther than the ceiling. Something seemed to hinder my "trips."

"Why is it that other people can travel to all sorts of places, even other planets, and all I can do is hover!" I groaned. It was terribly frustrating.

I had to be content with a different practice. During the half-sleep stage of dreaming I often became aware that I was reading pages of "divine information." Just when I tried to consciously focus on a sentence or two I'd wake up. Desperately longing to share these experiences with someone, I prayed for a kindred connection.

On Halloween night, 1976, I had a glimmer of hope.

Gerry and his wife had gone out with another couple and I was home babysitting. When they all returned they were squealing with excitement and Teresa looked like she'd seen something more than a Halloween ghost.

"I'm not the one who saw it but I don't know how I missed it," she said, shaking her head slowly. "It was right there, hovering above the traffic lights."

"Saw what? What are you talking about?" I looked at Teresa's friend Linda who was gesturing frantically.

"I have never believed in those things but we checked with the police, and they said that people all along the coast of Florida and Georgia spotted something unexplainable," Terry said, shaking her head. "Linda, you tell it. You're the one who saw it."

"*Please*, Linda. What did you see?" I begged.

Linda was beside herself with excitement. She paced

the floor nervously and started to spill out the story.

"All my life I've wanted to see a UFO. I'd hear other people say they witnessed those things and I never expected that I'd ever be so lucky. But there it was, a pulsating light that rested above the intersection. It was huge! Then it just whisked away!"

I was spellbound. It didn't matter if the sighting could be confirmed. I was more interested in Teresa's reaction. Her no-nonsense intellectual reasoning had just been shaken and she trusted Linda's sanity. Perhaps now I could talk to both of these women about extra-terrestial matters?

To my dismay Linda made herself scarce and Teresa just wasn't receptive. Even tales of a UFO weren't enough to bridge the gulf between our metaphysical experiences. My extended stay-over was creating a strain in the household and if I valued Gerry and Teresa as friends, I'd have to find somewhere else to live.

The gypsy lifestyle had deteriorated into nothing more than being a hobo. Some of the places where I bunked were dreary and dark. My parents had offered to buy me a second-hand car for transportation and I picked the most dilapidated model on the lot. It was all I deserved.

Every time I got a job it only lasted a week. The car broke down continuously; sometimes it quit in the middle of the highway. I tried hard to maintain the Buddhist philosophy to "be here now": the practice of observing one's life experience from an impersonal and unaffected viewpoint. It was much harder to do without sympathetic Questers to encourage me. Defeat and despair closed in on me.

Suicide wasn't for cowards, I reasoned. It was for the brave souls who knew that the "other side" was the ultimate goal. I wasn't brave enough to instigate my own transition. Turning my face to the grey wall of my dingy apartment, I agonized over my burdensome karma. Was there such a thing as terminal karma, I wondered.

"Oh God, where are you?" I sobbed. "Why is the path so hard? Look at me. I've become like one of those Bowery bums who show up at missions for soup along with a little preaching! I almost wish I knew a few of those backward Christians, just to talk to somebody."

It was an unlikely possibility. The few Christians I did run into always backed away fearfully whenever I mentioned reincarnation or cosmic awareness. I felt like I wanted to go home but I wasn't really sure where home was anymore. I couldn't face my parents. They'd done too much for me already.

Finally two jobs opened for me to teach in the morning and moonlight at a 24-hour day care center. At night I watched divorcees stumble drunkenly through the door to pick up dirty, sore-infested children who cried incessantly. Sometimes I peered over the cribs and whispered to the fretful infants, "I know how you feel, little ones. Earth is the real hell. We're all looking for the great escape."

One day my boss called to me from his office, "I have an errand to do. Want to ride along?"

It would be a welcome relief to get out of that environment for awhile. Those poor kids didn't even have a piano to provide them with comforting music.

"Sure. Let's go." I climbed into his van and stared out the window. "At least I practiced birth control all these years," I mumbled.

When we arrived at a carpenter's home my boss discussed cabinet measurements and I sat alone in the kitchen. There were some health food items stacked on the table and I realized that I'd been a lousy vegetarian. (When you're hungry you'll eat whatever somebody offers).

The carpenter's wife was a woman in her forties and she introduced herself as Sunny. I mentioned the food staples on her table and she handed me a dried slice of pineapple. We exchanged a few New Age passwords and I suspected that my soul would get some nourishment at the same time.

"Would you like me to play the piano for you?" Sunny asked abruptly. "It's what I do for people. Come, sit down over here and I will play whatever I pick up from you spiritually."

This was something new. I thought of the precious little children at the day care and wondered if Sunny could visit them sometime. She led me to a high-backed chair and I rested my head while she performed an impromptu serenade. Strains of celestial music filled the room and haunting melodies of forgotten memories seemed to emerge. I began to cry.

"I'm home. At last, I'm home," I murmured. It had been so long since anyone had touched my soul.

Sunny smiled sweetly and asked me what I was feeling. I couldn't find the words. Her husband had completed his business with my boss and it was time to leave. Reluctantly I rose to my feet and thanked the woman for her musical therapy. I felt impressed to ask her about a name I hadn't dared to mention until now.

"Have you ever heard of Saint Germain?" I asked cautiously.

"Why yes! He works closely with me. Saint Germain presides over the Aquarian religions." Sunny hugged me enthusiastically. "Promise we'll get together soon."

"You can count on it!" I ran to catch up with my

impatient boss.

I couldn't wait to see Sunny again. A New Age master had condescended to contacting me through a Ouija board once, and now I was making friends with one of Saint Germain's disciples!

6

Soul Mate

Sunny and I were quite a team. We drove from Orlando to Daytona once a week for meditations and past-life regressions at a beachside condominium. The couple who lived together there were students of Summit Lighthouse, an organization headed by a woman called Mrs. Prophet. So much of what she was teaching was identical to what Sunny already knew cosmically. (Saint Germain was the Summit's patron master at the time).

Sunny knew that Mrs. Prophet was regathering the members of King Arthur's Court! We were all mystified by the women's similarities and the men argued over which one of them was Merlin reincarnated.

It was funny how I had to commute to Daytona to find Questers like these. If I'd known that group when I lived with Sally I could have lived closer to the beach. I decided to pay her a visit.

Something was different about Sally. She seemed

radiant.

"I guess you'll be a married lady again and soon from the looks of you," I said. "Where's your fiance'?"

"I know you'll find this hard to believe. He's staying at a hotel." Sally twirled a lock of hair dreamily.

I stared at my friend incredulously. We'd travelled in the fast lane ever since we were in high school yet somehow I sensed that her boyfriend's location was her own idea.

"We aren't going to sleep together until we get married. It just had to be that way. If John can't handle it then I guess we won't get married."

"Come on, Sally! It's me, remember? You can tell me . . . is this the old ploy to trap a guy into security? What if John bolts and looks for somebody else? How can you be so calm about this?" John had practically been a permanent fixture when I moved out but I certainly didn't expect this turn-around.

"I'm calm because I'm trusting Jesus. Elissa, I got saved. Jesus is real. I want to have a real marriage in Christ."

I straightened stiffly in my chair and waited for the other shoe to drop. Sally didn't pressure me or try to convince me of anything. She just said she'd pray for me. That seemed harmless enough so I thanked her for her kind thoughts and left.

"Poor John," I sighed. "I'll bet he's completely bewildered."

The next time I went to Daytona with Sunny I neglected to call Sally. Instead I sat magnetized by the latest news from my Lighthouse friends. They'd seen a preview of an incredible movie with special effects and cosmic innuendoes.

"It's fantastic! Wait 'till you see this movie!" they

exclaimed. "It will definitely cause a worldwide revival of mysticism."

They said it was called *Star Wars*.

The new film hit our area like a hurricane. Throngs of "Trekkies" stood in line for hours to see the movie over and over again. The first time I watched it the credits were rolling and I said to my boyfriend, "Let's not leave. I want to see it again." Russ nodded mechanically.

My boyfriend designed light-and-sound systems as a hobby. As he sat hyponotically in front of the screen he whispered to me, "There really *is* a future for me. I knew I had been given these talents for a reason."

For a while I was sure that Russ could be instrumental in helping Sunny with the musical plays she had written. Their New Age theme, like the one called "Atlantis Rises," would need expert assistance. Sunny wanted to compile her plays into a lyrical "third testament." I tried hard to accept her idea but somehow it seemd a bit too presumptuous to call it a third *testament*. Besides, Russ was behaving weirdly, dressing in black and collecting serpent symbols. He could get into the occult *without* me.

Once we attended a Summit meditation at the beach and sat down quietly. The group was chanting, "I am a being of violet fire, I am the purity God desires."

The intensity grew and I felt hot and squirmy. The candle danced light across the faces of the chanters dressed in lavendar and sky blue clothing and I strained for fresh air.

"Sunny, I'm sorry. I have to get out of here," I gasped hoarsely. "You can stay if you like."

Sunny nodded with understanding and we excused ourselves. She had one of her migraines anyway so we set out for the long road home.

"I wish I could explain what happened back there," I groped for words. "Sometimes I feel like there are some boundaries. Even Russ has gotten too far into the psychic side of things."

"I know, dear. That's why it's so important to discern the differences. So many people get lost in the dark and it's such a thin line," Sunny explained. "You know, a lot of people think I've lost my balance, too!"

We laughed with one another as we neared Orlando. It was true — many of my own New Age friends criticized her for some of her interpretations. But I always protectively defended Sunny. She was so kind-hearted, so loving. She even had an explanation of Lucifer, the fallen angel. He had merely turned from the "light," and instead of hating him, we should reach out to him with love and compassion. Lucifer was just a mirror image of God's angels and mankind needed to restore him to wholeness. Joy and laughter would protect us from the dark entities, not suspicion and fear. Why couldn't fundamentalists see that? And why were some Questers so confused about the difference in spirit guides?

Sunny dropped me off at my apartment. Closing the car door I remembered another meditation being held in town.

"It's at the New Age bookstore on the full moon. Want to go with me?"

"I'll think it over first," Sunny winced. "My husband has been complaining that I'm never home anymore. You know how he gets!"

She drove away and I sympathized with her. Her husband had initially shown interest in cosmic awareness but he grew defiant and eventually rejected all of it.

"What's the matter with these men, anyway?" I griped

under my breath. "Either they trick you into thinking they're part of the movement and then back out of it or they go off the deep end."

I turned the key to my door and called it a night.

When the moon swelled to its fullness I drove to the meditation alone. Twenty of us assembled on the patio adjacent to the cosmic bookstore and positioned our cushions in a ring around the visiting guru who was actually an American who had travelled to Tibet for his training. He arrived with a flourish of orange robes and carried a large pipe-shaped musical instrument from the Himalayas. When he blew the signal for the meditation to begin the group laughed at its foghorn tune and our leader made a few off-color jokes. A nervous tittering erupted among the meditators as we were told to find a meditating partner. I didn't see Sunny in the shadows, and even though I had spotted a few friends (one was a musician who had gone to the Philippines for psychic surgery on his knee), I was startled when a stranger to my right whispered a breathy command, "Face me."

He was very young, blonde and wore the Oriental symbol of *yin* and *yang* on a golden pendant. Dressed in drawstring lounging pants and a gauzy shirt open at the neck, he seemed to luminate under the tropical trees that cast shadows on the plaza. Hypnotically I turned to sit cross-legged in front of him. The meditation proceeded. His name was Neil and for the next hour I was under his spell. I was so absorbed by his golden hair that when the meditation was over I found myself inviting him for a walk.

He held my hand and we spoke of our dreams for a New World. He would get his medical career established in Grenada and hoped to join the mystics rumored to live in South America.

As we talked we made our way barefoot through a lush jungle of trees in an unfamiliar part of the park. When I looked up I saw the garden gazebo I had dreamed of many years ago. Two husbands had come and gone and here I was, standing next to a fair-haired youth who seemed to say, "It is I."

I had found the man of my dreams and I quickly terminated my relationship with my old boyfriend. I began a new one with a man ten years my junior.

We had a summer of wild abandon and uninhibited fantasies. We talked of marriage and teamwork in the New Age and I thought I had truly found my life-long soul mate.

One of his practices, however, disturbed me. He liked to do mysterious rituals of white magic for prosperity. When I watched him pour salt in the shape of a circle under the moonlight, I declined to participate. My refusal annoyed him but he had already confided in me too much. Not many women would have tolerated his fantasies. (While trying to find a balance between the dual natures of masculinity and femininity, he experimented with cross-dressing).

By the end of the summer I had confirmed his virility. I was pregnant. After twelve years of determined birth control, I had "left it up to God" and now I was entangled in a web of confusion and bewilderment. I was still legally married to my second husband and Neil couldn't quit medical school to take care of a baby.

The logical solution was abortion. Neil offered to pay half of the cost.

While I awaited my turn in the clinic a dozen other women sat twisting their hair or stared into space. I tried to cheer up everyone around me with "every baby should be wanted."

To a selected few I shared the New Age justification for abortion. "The breath of life is always considered the beginning of life," I told them. "Besides, psychics report that unborn souls of babies return to the astral plane and await another incarnation or may be joined by the mother when she passes over to the other side." It didn't quell the sadness in their eyes, but I urged the other women not to succumb to guilt.

I was puzzled, however, by the young woman who was married and confessed that she didn't know why she was there except that babies change a couple's lifestyle and she liked hers just fine without children.

The procedure was brief but worse than I expected. Tearfully I said goodbye to my baby. Neil waited in the recovery room.

"Well, after this, I'll probably come back as a rock in my next life," I shrugged to my boyfriend. Of course, neither of us believed that a human soul could reincarnate into animals or inanimate objects, only other humans on a higher level. But somehow the act I had just committed seemed very grave in spite of my aloof attitude.

Neil took off for school that fall and I needed to find another place to live. Sunny knew of a woman who had been evicted from her last dwelling and introduced me to Sarah. It wouldn't be the first time I'd accept a living arrangement with a stranger and this woman certainly was strange.

7

From Karma to Grace

Sarah was a Jewish trance medium. She had worked out of famed Cassadaga, a spooky community for spiritualists in Central Florida.

Tom Petty, a rock star, immortalized Cassadaga in song. It is the kind of place where teenagers go on a stormy night to scare themselves. On grey and blustery days in Cassadaga the Spanish moss beckons eerily from dead trees and mediums jealously argue over who will get the next customer for a reading. Two predictions I'd received from a medium there had come true already: I would meet a red-haired man and there was a baby in my future.

The lighting expert was the redhead but he and the baby were gone.

Sarah arrived with three Persian cats, each bearing cosmic-sounding names. My Siamese cat crouched threateningly. Sarah and I split expenses for the cheap duplex and settled down. The cats hissed a lot.

That Christmas we both lost our jobs. It was the first time in my life I'd ever been fired — for refusing a cut in salary. We couldn't even afford oil for the heater and I was worried about how we'd last the winter with no income.

Sarah gave readings and meditation classes in the Florida room to pay her bills and I was asked to consider starting my own school. The children missed me!

"We think it's a shame that you were let go like that," the mothers said, nodding in agreement.

"My son cries for Miss Elissa every morning," another anguished.

"How long would it take you to get your own school together?" they all wanted to know.

I was overwhelmed by their loyalty. If I could figure a way to find financial support, maybe I could really do it my way. After several meetings with area Montessorians, I collected the necessary information I needed as an administrator and waited for the next step.

My parents offered to loan me the money.

"Are you sure? I haven't been able to pay back anything so far." I cringed at the thought of heaping debts with no assurance of a return.

"This is different," mother insisted. "This is an investment."

Within two weeks I bought second-hand Montessori equipment, gathered assorted materials and located a nearby church for operating room. I was on my way to succeeding for a change.

Meanwhile Sarah and I were fighting more than our cats. I was turning into a neat freak and she couldn't be bothered with mundane chores. Frequently I avoided her séances and psychometric classes where objects are psychically "read."

Since the school term was nearly over, I knew I needed to spend more time looking for a permanent location for my Aquarian Academy. Sarah often stayed out of my way.

My meeting with a metaphysical Nazi educator had been disappointing to say the least. I certainly didn't want a Nazi for a collaborator in my school. No matter how advanced or enlightened some of us were, there were always those who gave spiritualism a bad reputation. Sarah seemed to find a few of her own.

The vitamin therapist was one of those.

He arrived with a masseur's folding table and a case of vitamin bottles. I secretly envied Sarah because I knew she was going to get a massage and a new supply of vitamins. (How I had loved the foot massager who came for a reading once!) But this therapist had unorthodox methods.

He told Sarah to get aboard the table and then proceeded to place the bottles directly on different places of her back.

Peering into her room, I asked cynically, "What's that supposed to do?"

The therapist explained. "It isn't really necessary to ingest the vitamins; their vibrations will be absorbed through the skin."

I quickly remembered an errand and left.

Another stranger followed Sarah home one night and it was the only time I ever locked my bedroom door.

He had long hair and wild eyes that I had never seen except in pictures of Charles Manson. He babbled about triple sixes and the Beast and he vacillated between being passionately attracted to Sarah and then berating her for being a Jezebel. I sat on the sofa and watched him

dart erratically around the living room like a caged
animal. When he emerged from the bathroom wearing a
white robe and brandishing a wooden staff, I didn't know
what to expect.

"Don't you think I'd make a good shepherd?" he challenged.

I backed away from him cautiously and nodded.

"Sure . . . very convincing!"

"Have you read Revelation in the Bible?" His face was
inches away from mine and his dark brown eyes glim-
mered.

"Not much," I confessed. "Uh, I think you'd better
check on Sarah now. I'm getting sleepy."

Behind my locked door I wondered if I'd just met one
of those Jesus freaks from a Christian cult. There was no
telling whether he was a mystic, a Christian or a com-
bination of both. I slept fitfully that night and when
Sarah knocked on my door she admitted that the man
also had frightened her. She'd asked him to leave.

"Thank God," I heaved gratefully. It was all I had to do
just keeping my school afloat without worrying that we'd
be bludgeoned to death in our sleep. The image of the
shepherd's staff faded with my growing responsibilities.

I had started a scrapbook of notes pertaining to my
school and one article was all about the New Age child.
Marcus Bach, staff writer for Unity Magazine and an
uncle to the author of *Jonathan Livingston Seagull,*
answered "Questions on the Quest."

Bach explained that this is a buzz-word in the catch-
phrase category that suggests insights "typical of our
thinking as we rush headlong toward the twenty-first
century."

"The term may have as much to do with 'new age
parents' as with their offspring . . ."

He listed several points to describe the New Age belief that "children in our modern era often reflect a recall of previous lives ... (they rapidly mature) in body and soul, (and) psychic introspections ..."

Bach attributed some of these abilities to the "higher perceptivity on the part of mom and dad as well as the child."

Then he explained wonder children, or prodigies, born with above-normal talents.

"The word 'genius' originally means 'a spirit in charge of a person or place,' and the word gradually came to be applied directly to the person."

In another item from "Questions on the Quest," Bach confirmed my basic attitudes toward superstitious Christians who insisted on a belief in the devil which "goes all the way to half-forgotten faiths which believe that God and Satan were constantly engaged in a battle for the sovereignty of the human soul, to fundamental Christianity that presents a God, who paradoxically, loved the world so much that he gave his only begotten Son to be crucified and save all wayward souls."

Armed with clippings and quotes to support my position, I was amazed at how many adults were receptive to metaphysics. Their children simply enjoyed the exercises in yoga and they responded innocently to the "quiet times" of reflective meditations. Aquarian Montessori Academy could survive without big-time collaborators.

During that time my father sent me a book on "Chantomatics" which listed formulae for prosperity. The words looked like a foreign language and there was no way to know how to pronounce them correctly. Pointing them out to another New Ager, I laughed and said facetiously, "What if I'm conjuring up some evil spirits with this mumbo-jumbo!"

It was a joke, of course. We'd heard stories about magical incantations and voodo rituals taking place in various parts of the world but we were more civilized than that.

However, just to be safe, I discarded the book and the practice. Instead, I begged my mother for her jade statue of Buddha and placed him on a small table next to an old incense burner that my father had once used in his meditations.

The Buddha was a beautiful ornament in my home but he soon lost his charm. I wanted to know more about *all* the avatars and this master was too cold and impersonal.

Then there was Krishna who seemed to demand a lot of discipline and I wasn't so sure I could associate with men who shaved their heads and made women walk several paces behind them.

"Maybe I ought to look up some information on Jesus," I mused. "He was our latest example of the Christ and I don't really know that much about him."

The logical source was anything that contained the lesser-known facts. I purchased a copy of the *Aquarian Gospel of Jesus the Christ* by Levi and made a mental note to study the secrets that had been revealed telepathically to an individual who had access to the Akashic records.

Both Sarah and Sunny seemed to know more about ways to tap into the esoteric accounts but these hidden records of karma and universal mind were plainly available in the form of a book. Sunny planned to move to a mountain retreat and Sarah and I were constantly at odds with one another. A book seemed much more accessible.

I prayed for a little more peace and quiet in our apartment so I could enjoy my new book without interruption.

What resulted was a terrible scene with my roommate — and a showdown. One of us would have to leave. This time I was staying put.

When the dust settled I did a thorough job of housecleaning and stood triumphantly admiring the spoils of my victory. I had the place to myself. I knew I'd have to select another roommate from the waiting list of wandering friends but at least it was quiet for a while. I got out my Aquarian explanation of Jesus and enjoyed the sunlight pouring into the vacated Florida room.

The reported account of the missing years of the Bible deliciously peppered the text. Jesus had visited many masters of other lands and gleaned the wisdom that would help him when he became Christ. This was certainly more interesting than the regular Bible, although I had to admit that I hadn't read much of that one except for trying to verify my beliefs in reincarnation.

The main character in any novel can really keep the reader intrigued and the more I read about Jesus in New Age terms the more I felt attracted to him.

When the account of his suffering at the cross was described, I began to understand the real sacrifice of this "lamb of God come to take away the sins of mankind." So many religions demanded blood sacrifices throughout history but I began to perceive that this servant of God had willingly and obediently offered himself as a substitute for man's karma. God had realized how helplessly fallible mankind continues to be and, for all man's attempts to become as God, he always fell short of perfection on his own. He would always be guilty of those failings. As I read the words describing the nails and the blood I felt as if I were right there at the cross, weeping with the women beneath him. For an instant I considered that I probably had lived during those times and had actually known the master. But my mind and heart seemed to be in the midst of an intellectual and emotional conflict.

If Jesus had come to earth to offer the gift of grace, the unearned and undeserved escape from the karmic wheel, then as one of his followers I wouldn't have had to return to face subsequent karma! Like an enormous machine that had disengaged its gears, intellectual understanding groaned with surrender. In a single moment my heart virtually broke for the beloved Son of God who laid down his life as a covering for my sins. There was no denying it, karma or no karma, I had truly sinned in this life and I begged to be forgiven.

Crying deep sobs from my uttermost soul, I wept aloud, "My Lord, my Lord! I'm so sorry. Please forgive me."

The events of my life flashed to memory as if a newsreel was spinning vividly before my eyes. I saw the countless times of selfishness, tremendous spiritual pride and outright idolatry to other masters. These revelations seared through my consciousness and pierced me with shame and regret. I realized that I had not only been guilty of daring to make myself as wise as God himself, I had willingly participated in the murder of an unborn child. As I repented from my selfish pride and disobedience to the most High Creator, I wasn't even aware that I had become born again, saved from God's wrath. All I knew was that I'd been forgiven and Jesus was my new master.

For days I could hardly stand up. The recognition of God's love overwhelmed me so greatly that I often fell to my knees and thanked him again and again. Also, I had an unexplainable urge to be baptized. That weekend I drove to the beach for a private ceremony between God and me.

On a deserted stretch of sand I made my way to the water's edge. Reverently praying to my Lord, I committed my life to him. It was an act born from desire. No one had approached me with the news that it was a commandment of obedience. I stood with the water at waist-level and whispered, "Jesus, I want to belong to you forever. Thank you for your forgiveness." Bending my knees, I submerged my body under the waves and let the water wash over me. I stood up and praised God.

I felt clean — from my soul to my skin.

Somehow I had the feeling that life would never be the same.

8

"Cosmic Christian"

In May of 1978 I became a Christian. Buddha would have to move over.

I desperately wanted to represent my new Master with a picture or a figurine. I didn't want the typical Sunday school version of Jesus. I made a trip to my local cosmic bookstore and asked for a picture of Christ.

I was handed an artistic rendition of a man with long hair but the caption read "Lord Maitreya."

"Excuse me, but this isn't Jesus Christ," I complained to the owner. "This is Maitreya."

"Yes, but you see Maitreya is the Christ of the Aquarian Age. Jesus was the Christ for the Piscean Age," the shopowner answered smiling sweetly.

I knew this was not the precious Jesus I had come to know but I purchased the picture anyway and set upon finding a portrait that suited me better. Eventually I did find one, by Sallman, where Jesus was holding a lamb in his arms. Celestial colors swirl around the Savior who stands atop the globe of Earth. With the colored lights painted on the canvas, friends teased me and called it "the disco Jesus." But now I had a picture of my Master.

Wherever I went all I could talk about was Jesus. My New Age friends did not share my enthusiasm.

"You won't turn into one of those fundamentalists, will you?" one sneered.

"Oh, you're a Jesus Freak this year. Super," another yawned.

"Just don't tell me that you'll start taking the Bible literally or anything," still another glared. "After all, lots of people have Jesus as their Master, but you're a New Ager. You could be an Aquarian Christian."

That seemed to make sense. The gospel according to Levi contained the clues of this age as one of "splendor and of light, because it is the home age of the Holy Breath; and the Holy Breath will testify anew for Christ, the Logos of eternal Love." The Holy Breath was called Visel, or Goddess of Wisdom. She told Levi, "You shall publish not to men the lessons of the Christ of ancient times," but of the "Spirit Age."

I was a New Age woman. I would be a Cosmic Christian. My new label would identify me as an enlightened follower of the Nazarene. This way I could embark upon a mission of bridging the gap between mysticism and mainline Christianity. It all seemed so simple. The New Age seekers were still laboring under their karma without knowing they could be set free through Jesus. The fundamentalists had accepted Jesus but didn't know the power and insights of deeper interpretation. If I could find a way to blend those revelations then perhaps both sides would welcome me.

My old ankh necklace would surely turn away dyed-in-the-wool Christians and a plain cross wasn't suitable, either. Besides, I couldn't seem to hang on to any of the crosses I'd received as gifts. Invariably each one fell off the chain or got snagged and broke. So I called my jeweler friend for an appointment.

"I want a custom-made symbol," I told her.

We sketched some ideas and finally settled on just the right design. The circle with a cross beneath it symbolized the insignia of "woman." In the middle of the circle we drew wavy lines for the zodiac sign of Aquarius. When I returned to pick up my new religious symbol I was mildly disappointed that the cross looked more like a plus sign instead of a Calvary cross but it would have to do. Now when a curious individual commented on my jewelry I would be ready to launch into my campaign to unify believers of all persuasions.

My first mission was to contact Sally. She would be ecstatic to know that I'd become a Christian, too, only now I could broaden her horizons. Sally was in the middle of her wedding arrangements. She wanted me to know that her fiance', a staunch Catholic who had never seen a need to become "born again," had given his heart and life to Jesus. He even attended church with her. I listened politely and then shared a few of my insights. She became noticeably quiet then issued a gentle warning.

"Elissa, I'm so glad you accepted Jesus Christ as your Savior. But I really think you should be careful about some of the things you're trusting in. Forgive me, but I think you've been deceived. I'll keep praying for you."

I smiled to myself. Sally was content to take the Bible literally but if it hadn't been for her prayers I might not have come to know Jesus at all. I thanked her for her prayers and went back to my cosmic books.

In my father's library there was one about Jesus that dad thought I might enjoy. It was called *The Mystical Life of Jesus* published in 1929 by H. Spencer Lewis, the Rosicrucian. On the inside cover was a drawing of my beloved Lord. This caption read, "Jesus, the Aryan Gentile."

Could it be possible that Jesus really wasn't a Jew after all? I scanned the chapters that spoke of "hidden facts" about Christ's birth, his death and his resurrection. Secret activities with the Essenes influenced most of what *really* happened and I was a little confused about the Bible stories I had heard somewhere in my childhood. Then, on page 245, I saw a symbol that was described as one of the most sacred designs of Tibetan monks, Buddhist priests and early gnostic Christians. It was a reversed swastika.

There can't be a connection, I reasoned to myself. I dismissed the idea.

One afternoon I found a box of checks in my post office box. After taking them home I realized that the name of the owner was different even though the address was mine. I called the man's phone number and explained the mix-up. He thanked me, got directions to my house and I waited for his arrival. The logo on the checks read "What the World Needs is Jesus." I looked forward to sharing my mystic views of Christ with the man.

When he arrived, I learned that the man's wife was also a Montessori teacher! I showed him one of my "Aquarian Montessori" business cards. He was very quiet as I explained how my father was a Rosicrucian and had the gift of healing.

The stranger looked at me carefully and said slowly, "You may not be aware of this but Satan can counterfeit the gifts of the Holy Spirit."

I felt my temperature rising. "What are you saying? That my father is in league with the devil? My father has never had anything but the highest regard for things of God," I angrily challenged.

"Perhaps he is very sincere but your father has been deceived."

The stranger turned to leave and he noticed the large ceramic astrology wheel that decorated my wall. "I'd get rid of that if I were you," he said ominously.

The man left and I stood there in frustration. It would take a lot of doing to enlighten these fundamentalists. My whole body was quaking but I refused to give up. I would have to learn to be more patient with the uneducated Christians.

Then I thought that perhaps I would find consolation among my New Age buddies in a nearby town. I hadn't seen that group of Questers since my conversion and I wanted to share my news with them.

To my amazement nine out of ten of them reported being born again to Jesus Christ! They hadn't collectively attended some lecture; each had experienced salvation independently of the others. And even more unsettling, all but one had absolutely no interest in blending metaphysics with Christianity. In fact, some of them talked about cleaning up their lifestyles. They wanted marriage instead of casual dating or living with their lovers!

"What's going on?" I thought. These were the same friends who had constructed pyramids in their apartments, who had recalled past lives and had spent hours talking about the dream of a New World order. Now they wouldn't even talk to me about reincarnation. Instead, they were attending regular churches and having Bible study groups in their homes. They'd become *fundamentalists!*

It seemed like a good idea to get into the Bible myself. I dusted off an old Bible that I never read much and began with the Gospel of John. It was as if veils lifted from my eyes and the words came alive in my heart. I flipped from page to page and heard my Savior telling me, *"No man can serve two masters,"* and *"Take heed that no one leads you astray, for many will come in my name, saying 'I am the Christ.'"*

Jesus spoke of the devil who *"has nothing to do with the truth, because there is no truth in him. When he lies, he speaks according to his own nature, for he is a liar and the father of lies."*

Hungrily I started searching the Scriptures. In Exodus I read the historical account of Moses pleading in behalf of his people that Pharaoh would release them from slavery. Moses had been brought up in the temples of Egypt and had enjoyed its wealth. He had been surrounded by the wizards and sorcerers all his life. When he left it all behind him and joined the shepherds of his Hebrew heritage, he was at a loss for words. *"Who am I that I should go to Pharaoh?"* Moses asked the Lord God.

The Lord assured his doubtful servant that he would not have to go alone but that the hand of the Lord God of Israel would be upon Moses and miracles would convince the Pharaoh.

It was an old story I'd seen on reruns of *The Ten Commandments* several times. But now I began to see what Jesus meant by *"false teachers working signs and wonders."* The Egyptian wise men could duplicate almost every one of the miracles God worked through Moses and I knew whose side God was on. Mastery of the psychic arts was no indication that a practitioner was serving God.

I read the Book of Revelation and discovered clues describing the Antichrist. The more I studied the Bible the more mysteries were uncovered.

When Sarah called to tell me that she had also experienced salvation in Jesus, I rejoiced with her. She, too, couldn't wait to get baptized and had splashed tap water all over herself in celebration. But when she described her "conversion" experience I got very edgy.

Apparently Jesus had come to her while she was in a trance. He spoke to her concerning his worldwide appearance, how he would come out of Rome. He would be blonde and he would communicate to thousands of people over a telecommunications system. He would enter buildings and leave them without visible explanation.

Bracing myself for her reaction, I spoke softly but with determination.

"Sarah, I know you really believe that you saw Jesus. But what you have just told me is a very good description of the Antichrist. You got good information but it was about the wrong man."

Psychics do not like to be corrected. It insults their egos and their accuracy is very important to them. Sarah hung up on me and it was several months before we spoke again. The next time, we agreed to attend a prophecy lecture being held at a local church.

When we entered the building we sat down together and waited for the film strip. We were told to open the complimentary Bibles to follow along with the speaker. Sarah fidgeted in her seat and looked for an exit.

"This isn't at all what I expected," she whispered hoarsely. "Besides, I know all the stuff that's in this psychically." Sarah threw the Bible back onto its place behind the pew and left in a hurry.

My heart grieved. If Sarah actually *could* know what was in the Bible without reading it, she would have known that consulting mediums and seers was an abomination to the Lord.

It was becoming more obvious that New Agers had their own Jesus and not the Jesus Christ of the Bible, the Son of God. I didn't want any other Jesus than the one who said, *"Behold, I am coming with the clouds, and every eye shall see him, every one who pierced him; and all tribes of the earth will wail on account of him. I am the Alpha and the Omega, who was and is to come, the Almighty."*

9

Starting Over

Had I still been thinking like a New Ager, I would have considered 1979 as my "closing cycle year" on a numerology chart. The end of that decade proved to be the beginning of an entirely new direction but this time with Christ charting the course.

The first order of business was to give my school a new name. "Aquarian Montessori Academy" was no longer appropriate. I chose "*Agape* Montessori" to honor the kind of sacrifical love exemplified in Christ. "*Agape*" (which rhymes with "copy") is a Greek word which is often mispronounced, and whenever I heard anyone refer to the school's name as if it were a slack-jaw condition, I nodded in agreement. Certainly the ways of God left me "gaping, as in wonder," as my teaching philosophy underwent transformation.

The basic Montessori techniques remained intact but I enthusiastically made a few revisions. The standard procedure for a lesson in handwashing became a tender ritual of footwashing. Since the purpose was to serve rather than be served, little children asked each other if they would like to have their feet washed and it would be up to the individual if he wanted to return the service. Sandy little bare feet were treated to gentle rinsing and soothing lotion and it was precious to see the bonding friendships develop. At Easter we didn't dye eggs; rather, we waved palm fronds and sang hosannas. Even Christmas carols sounded sweeter and it was the best year of my teaching career.

The matter of my marital limbo also needed to be resolved. I would either have to get a legal divorce or attempt a reconciliation with my estranged husband. Longing to share my new found faith with Rich, I thought it was a miracle when he agreed to return to Florida. Rich had other ideas.

Instead of my apartment acting as the setting for a reconciliation, I learned that it was only meant to serve as a pit stop for my husband. Hiding from creditors while waiting for a position in a brewery over fifty miles away, Rich didn't seem too concerned about how I could maintain my school while he commuted on weekends.

When he let it slip that he'd been living with another woman on the west coast of Florida, he wasted no time escaping my reaction. I'd been set up all along and all I could do was look for a lawyer again. This time I had scriptural grounds for a divorce from an unbeliever.

The thought of climbing back on the dating merry-go-round seemed strangely uncomfortable. I had to be honest with myself. I wanted a Christian marriage or none at all. Without a stereo or a television to keep me company, I sat in my living room and wrapped my arms around my shoulders, rocking like a sobbing child.

"Oh, Jesus. You know me better than anyone. Every time I try to choose a man I always end up in a mess. This time I want you to do the picking. Please, I want to be married to someone who desires to know you better and who will want a traditional marriage."

Then, as if I thought God needed any help from me, I tried to hurry up the progress and went scouting for likely candidates from among the ex-New Agers who were now Christians. I sent a little note to one man who had expressed his need for a Christian wife and invited him to come over and listen to some of the gospel albums I'd been collecting. The note came back stamped "Undeliverable." I suspected the Lord's intervention and decided to wait on God as I had promised.

Practically under my nose was "the boy next door." He'd already been trying to put his life together after his marriage had deteriorated and when we commiserated over our failures our mutual friends called it the "rebound syndrome." Actually, I was so busy looking to distant possibilities that I didn't even notice how God was bringing about the desires of my heart. Les, or "Red" as his friends called him, had shoulder-length hair and a long shaggy beard. He wore bib overalls and hiking boots and fit the category of men which I had vowed never again to date. I'd had enough of "irresponsible hippie freaks" so I tried to throw him off course by witnessing. I wasn't certain about Red's religious beliefs but I noticed that he wore an ankh. When I commented on it, I hoped it would lead to an opportunity to share my testimony with him.

"I used to wear one of those," I began.

"Yeah, well, I'm sort of into King Tut," he said, giving his ponytail a flip.

"*Now* I'm into the King of Kings," I bluntly countered

and waited for a reaction. To my surprise Red was attracted to the light of the gospel more than I imagined. His mother had died several months earlier and he was still grieving her loss. He told me he was the only youngster in the family who had enjoyed going to church with her and he promised me he'd find her Bible. The next time we saw each other he handed me the book that had been passed down from his grandmother. Together we read the underlined passages that had meant so much to his mother. The first three verses in the fourteenth chaper of John were underscored in red pencil:

"Let not your heart be troubled; ye believe in God, believe also in me. In my Father's house are many mansions; if it were not so, I would have told you. I go to prepare a place for you. And if I go and prepare a place for you, I will come again, and receive you unto myself; that where I am, there ye may be also."

"I know my mother is in heaven," Red spoke softly. "She didn't fear death at all and I know her Bible was a comfort to her."

I could see the work of the Holy Spirit preparing Red's heart and presented the invitation to Christ, "You can be certain that you will see her again. Jesus wants your life, too, Red."

In brokenness and submission to God, Red gave his heart to Jesus Christ and wept with emotions that had been repressed for months, maybe even years. His moment of becoming born again occurred privately but when he joined me to attend a church service Red bolted out of his chair at the first altar call to make a public confession of his new faith.

It had been years since I had participated in a traditional communion service and for some unexplained reason I really wanted to be part of a ceremony that signified Christ's blood atonement. Since neither Red nor I were members of any church, we went to three different locations trying to find a church that observed communion. And that was all in one Sunday! At last, we found a church where a glimmering chalice graced the communion table and we solemnly stood in line to receive our portion. The significance of the new "passover" was made real to us and we exchanged glances of acknowledgement. On our way out of the church Red noticed something else about the event.

"The people there sure are friendly. We were strangers there, but not one of them frowned at my long hair."

During the "radical" days long hair had been a kind of personal flag of defiance. Within a very short time Red cut his hair and trimmed his beard but not to please anyone in particular. He just said, "Jesus is changing me on the inside; I decided that the outside needed a new look."

I was a bit relieved. Our friendship had blossomed into a serious relationship and it was time to introduce him to my parents. They were broadminded but they would definitely have a better impression of Red now that his hair was short.

Soon our wedding date arrived. We invited a few close friends to the simple ceremony. We asked for the standard vows to be read instead of writing a "conditional contract" and the minister gave us communion. Each of us felt like we'd never been married before and it was the first time either of us had looked upon a union as a reverent commitment.

After years of looking for the perfect "soul mate," I discovered that any relationship can hope for success only if Christ is at the center. My new husband and I embraced Christian priorities and wanted God's will. But Red was the one who more readily accepted the jolting news shortly after we were married.

There had been rumors that some drastic changes were about to take place in the church where I was holding class. I was nervous that these changes would affect my school and voiced my concern to the residing pastor. He assured me that I could continue at the location and I ended the term confidently expecting next year's enrollment.

However, a few weeks before the fall semester I was told that the church board had decided to organize its own day care. I was stranded without an alternative location.

I was incredulous when a member of the church confided that the church decision to oust "Agape Montessori" had been made months before.

Red had worked so diligently to prepare the building to meet regulation standards. Now our financial security was stripped from us.

The whole charade of honesty and professionalism in a church body was almost enough to drive us away from churches altogether. But at least we knew how to pray.

"God closed this door. Don't worry; He'll open another," Red comforted me. "You said you always wanted to write. Look, I'll take care of things; you can stay home and do that book you never had time for."

Was this a dream? I thought back to the time when I might have studied under the author Catherine Marshall. I hadn't "lived" enough to write anything then, but now I had more than a few ideas on inspirational topics. I had been putting together some pieces from other occult investigators.

We sold the Montessori equipment and I purchased an electric typewriter.

In 1980 I placed two ads in Christian magazines inviting the testimonies from others who looked for God through mysticism before finding the truth personified in Jesus Christ. Maybe others could contribute to the warnings to New Agers that the vision of worldwide brotherhood and religious unity was not just an Aquarian Age "Quest" — it was a plot to deify man's ego and revive the ancient temptation to listen to the serpent, "Surely God knows that when your eyes are open you shall be as gods, knowing both good and evil."

Over the months the responses were slow to arrive. I spent hours at the library and in Christian bookstores and studied the Bible eagerly. All during this time the Lord continued to sift the chaff from my life and set my feet on solid ground. I knew God had given me the most loving husband in the world and I wanted to thank the Lord by sharing his miracles in print.

I had no way of knowing how the Holy Spirit was leading countless others out of the slavery masquerading as religious enlightenment and that their stories and experiences were also miraculous — and very sobering.

But I was soon to find out.

10

Getting to Know
the Trinity Personally

Since I no longer had a teaching job to take most of my time, for the first few weeks I felt like a fish out of water. While the neighborhood children noisily made their way to the bus stop I retreated to my "office," a converted guest room, and cross-referenced my materials, typed and re-typed.

One night I was so exhausted that I just needed a fresh touch from the Lord. It seemed I'd done a lot of talking about him but hadn't spent much time communicating *with* him. Wearily easing into bed I sighed, "Jesus, just let me know you're there. I need more of you."

I drifted into half-sleep and in a dream beheld the image of my Saviour bathed in an iridescent blend of rose-gold, the color was exquisite. I noticed that he was wearing a white robe that seemed like soft linen draped over his head and shoulders. It was a curious vision for I had not pictured Jesus that way. I always thought of him

either with the crown of thorns or the victorious crown
for the King of Kings. Also, Jesus wasn't looking at me,
but his face was angled upwards as though he was
listening. The vision faded and I was content that Jesus
had honored my request to "just let me know he was
there."

Trying to interpret the glimpse I had just seen, I
considered that maybe he was listening to the Father.
Satisfied, I forgot about the dream until we had dinner
with another Christian couple.

"You know," I said, toying with my vegetables,
"Lately I've been so absorbed with Jesus that maybe I
have left out the Father."

Steve passed the rice and nodded. "I know just what
you mean. It was the same for me for quite a while after I
got saved. It was always Jesus, Jesus until I read in the
Bible that now we can go directly to the Father in prayer
through the Son. We'll look it up after dinner."

We found in John 16:26:

"In that day you ask in my name; and I do not say to
you that I shall pray the Father for you; for the Father
himself loves you, because you have loved me and have
believed that I came from the Father."

Years ago I had called God "Father," but his title
changed as my understanding of God diffused into
"Divine Mind," "Cosmic Consciousness," and "The
Force" or "Father-Mother." Eventually God became
"It." I once had ridiculed others who actually pictured
God as "some old man on a throne."

Yet Jesus always referred to the Almighty God as his
Father. He gave examples of the character and heart of
God as an earthly father who seeks to embrace and

nurture his children. Moments before Christ's arrest Jesus cried "Abba," the Aramaic word for father.

Now, as adopted children and heirs to God through Jesus Christ, we too could say, "Abba, Father." It was good again to call him Father.

Father, Son and Holy Ghost. God had revealed himself as Jesus and was now my heavenly father. But what about this Holy Ghost? During my brief exposure to a Methodist Sunday school they had mentioned this spooky apparition, but now I was hearing "Holy Spirit" on the lips of many Christians!

I'd found so much inner peace and joy as a Christian than I ever had during the years of meditation. So whatever was available to believers in Christ, I was ready!

A few months later Red announced that he wanted to bring some people home for dinner. He said that I should meet this couple since they were deeply involved in New Age religions and that they possibly would listen to my testimony. When I met them they reminded me of a family of left-over hippies caught in a time-capsule. (How quickly I'd forgotten my own hippie days of long hair and especially my own outlandish appearance when I was a New Ager!)

Red's new friends were named Josh and Rose. They had children with mystical and biblical names. Their five-year-old boy had hair to his waist (since Josh was convinced that cutting the hair "destroyed energy") and the two-year-old was not yet walking or talking. They were *strict* vegetarians and talked about their interest in a belief that one can live on water and energy in the air. I attempted to warn them about the serious damage they could be inflicting on their growing children, especially since the mother was nursing her two-year-old and was not receiving any protein herself.

Josh's fellow employees also criticized the dietary laws that he enforced upon his family, but Josh would not even accept our free offers of vitamins from the health food store.

They left our home and some time later one of the men from work asked us if we'd seen Rose lately. It had been several months since we'd been in touch with her or the family and Red and I assumed that we had offended Josh for not enthusiastically promoting his version of Christ. (Josh liked to pass out little decals of rainbows and stickers that read "The Christ will appear in '82).

"You should see her," our friend said, shaking his head. "She's as white as a ghost. She looks like a skeleton and her stomach looks like she's nine months pregnant, yet she says she isn't."

Josh's boss, a Christian, insisted that Rose be admitted to a hospital. Josh insisted that his wife go instead to a holistic doctor. Rose called me and said that upon orders from her husband she'd been treating her condition with enemas and juice fasting and even though she asked me to call a holistic center, she confided that she really didn't think this was the right thing for her to do.

I made the call to a local practitioner, described the conditions relayed to me and was told by the receptionist that the doctor would prescribe herbal juices and colonic irrigation!

Ultimately it was Josh's boss who demanded that Rose receive medical attention.

Rose was admitted to a Seventh-Day Adventist hospital where vegetarian items are offered along with other natural foods on the menu.

I was apprehensive, when I first went to see Rose.

Certainly she would need to renounce her involvement in what the Bible calls witchcraft, but it would be tough witnessing to her with her husband around. I decided I would pray first and get prepared with some scriptures.

The latest book I'd been reading was *The Challenging Counterfeit* by former psychic Raphael Gasson about his accounts on how cleverly demon spirits duplicate or impersonate souls and spirit guides. In addition to feeling immense grief for people like Rose who have been so viciously deceived, I started to feel inadequate to minister to this poor woman. Doubts tormented me.

"What makes you think *you* can do anything for Rose?" a sarcastic impression badgered me. "You're a sinful person yourself!" I recognized that our adversary continually accuses us before God (Rev. 12:10) but I was beginning to think I should just stay home.

Pleading with God to spare Rose and bring her to salvation and being consciously aware of my own protection by God's mercy during my own years of idolatry, I cried with deep sobs and praised the Savior fervently.

Shakily getting back to my feet I armed myself with my Bible and trembled with the awe of God's power all the way to the hospital.

Josh met me in the hall and embraced me, thanking me for coming to visit his wife. However, I was relieved when he said he had to go back to work for now I would have the opportunity to see Rose alone.

If I had not just experienced confirmation of God's assistance, I don't think I would have been prepared for what I saw when I entered Rose's room.

Rose was propped against her pillows. Her arms and legs were like spindles; shriveled skin flapped from her bony buttocks and her swollen abdomen was extended to its

limits. The translucent skin revealed a sickly yellow
fluid that had to be drained every other day. Her once-
lovely face was now deathly pale skin drawn tautly over
her skull and her eyes protruded from ashen sockets. I'd
heard descriptions of individuals who were completely
demon-possessed and her appearance fit all the characteristics. A shiver went down my spine and a wave of
nausea hit my stomach.

Rose smiled weakly and slowly lifted her hand to greet
me. I swallowed hard.

"Hang on, Rose. Help is on the way," I comforted.
"God will not abandon you."

With tears filling her eyes she whispered, "Oh, how I
need someone to talk to. Josh keeps saying that this is
my karma. He says I'm the personification of Venus but
so much of what he believes just doesn't feel right."

I squeezed her hand. "Rose, since I saw you last I've
found out a few more things about the occult. Don't fall
for that nonsense about Venus. The enemy tried to fool
another friend of mine with that one, too."

This poor woman had labored under the burden that
she was suffering now because it was her karma to take
upon herself "all the problems of the children in the
world," as Josh had insisted. I told Rose that only Jesus
could take our "karma" and that she could receive his
grace.

"Before I left the house, God directed me to a scripture just for you." I opened my Bible and read aloud the
beginning chapter of Isaiah 30. The concluding promise
was in verse 15:

*For thus saith the Lord God, the Holy One of Israel, In
returning and rest shall ye be saved; in quietness and in
confidence shall be your strength . . ."*

and in verse 18:

"Therefore will the Lord wait, that he may be gracious unto you, and therefore will he be exalted, that he may have mercy upon you: for the Lord is a God of judgement: Blessed are all they that wait for him."

I promised Rose I would come again, the next time with a Christian brother who had more experience in the deliverance ministry.

Meanwhile, the doctors puzzled over Rose's condition. They suspected a cancerous tumor but she was too weak for major surgery. Rose would need to gain some weight and receive medications until her illness could be accurately diagnosed.

As I drove home I trembled with the realization that Rose had not been brainwashed by any organized cult that withholds protein in order to starve the brain. She was the victim of the same philosophies I had studied which draw the seeker farther away from the truth of the gospel. A deep desire to become physically purified in order to elevate spiritual receptivity nearly killed her.

The next time I visited Rose I brought my friend who ministered deliverance. I braced myself when he began encouraging Rose to repent from all interest in the occult. I'd seen exorcisms on television but I didn't know what to expect.

Rose only cried softly as she surrendered her former attempts to know God. Her invitation to accept Jesus Christ's forgiveness came quietly, with obvious relief and exhaustion. God's mercy was great that day; Rose's frail body could not have withstood any more upheaval. The words of God's promise echoed in my thoughts, *". . . In returning and rest shall ye be saved; in quietness and in confidence shall be your strength."*

I continued to visit Rose until she was released a month later. I brought other Christian friends who reminded her to read her Bible in spite of the many books on mysticism that Josh kept leaving with her. One day Rose excitedly told me she had found something in one of Josh's books which he evidently had ignored:

"Whatever you do, don't go overboard on any philosophies which are not meant for intelligent Western people. The evanescent promises they make, and I must refer particularly to the cults of the East, all too often cause the victims to lose their sense of reality. . . I realize that this advice is useless to those who have been indoctrinated with elusive and fantastic expectations of achieving states of consciousness for which our body and mind are not intended. It is a mentally dangerous game which ensnares those who are not capable of thinking for themselves."

The author concluded, "A life time of research has pointed out to me that Almighty God created each one of us for a purpose; it is up to us to discover that purpose. Since we cannot get answers from *thin air*, we have been given the Bible, the infallible Word of God as our guide —STUDY IT!" (Norman W. Walker D. Sc. Ph.D., from "Colon Health: Key to a Vibrant Life," page 153. Woodside and Co., Phoenix, Arizona).

Rose had been fed everything but essential nutrients and the Bread of Life, the Bible. Her answers were indeed coming from thin air for Satan is called "*the prince of the powers of the air*" (Eph. 2:2).

The doctors had diagnosed pancreatitis, a condition common to alcoholics, yet neither Rose nor my father ever drank more than a glass of wine in a year. The doctor later removed some gallstones from her.

Months later Rose's color had returned, her body was filling out attractively and her countenance was radiant. She was reading her Bible and expressed a desire to find a cross to wear. In the meantime, she wore a Star of David. She had found her God, the Lord of Israel. Rose described all the tasty new foods she had included in her diet, and when I saw her last she promised not to let her husband influence her beliefs about God.

The Lord performed a living miracle in the life of our friend Rose and I learned about the work of the Holy Spirit. When Jesus ascended to his father he told his followers he would not leave them comfortless, but would send another — the Comforter, the Counselor, the Holy Spirit (John 14:16-18). He also promised his followers they would receive power from on high. I was now Christ's follower, a born-again Christian, and I'd experienced that promised power.

These days, whenever I don't know what or how to pray, I pray in the Spirit.

In the same way, the Spirit helps us in our weakness. We do not know what we ought to pray, but the Spirit Himself intercedes for us with groans and utterances that words cannot express" (Rom. 8:26).

The Trinity remains a mystery in the minds of men. Yet it is a mystery which God invites us to know personally — Father, Son and Holy Ghost.

The Lord is author of miracles and as the day approaches when Jesus Christ returns for his church the adversary continues to play out his last-ditch efforts to confuse and confound. The evidences of counterfeiting the supernatural of God have created similar "gifts" among occultists. They are disguised in modern packages. It was hardly a relief to discover I wasn't the only one to find this out.

11

Shocking Surprises From "Angels of Light"

"Red, I finally got a response from the ads!" I waved the envelope excitedly at my husband and we cheered as we anticipated the testimonies from other New Age drop-outs.

Quite candidly, I expected to hear from people who had experienced similar restlessness along the Quest as I had and that their stories would be mostly, "Well, I tried astrology, tarot cards, alpha levels, etc. and now I'm saved, amen."

Instead, this first letter made me realize just how severely we New Agers had been deceived. I knew I would be receiving chilling accounts from those who wrote me.

The respondent wrote of her experiences in a "mail-order" correspondence course and it named the organization that promised to enlighten the student. As I read the words, the page fluttered in my shaking hands.

"Five years ago I almost lost my life after studying the teachings of an organization called Astara. These teachings didn't make sense to me at first, but I found myself irresistibly drawn back to them over and over again. I remember the moment when everything suddenly fit together and made sense. It was like a divine revelation and my mind and body seemed flooded by a white light. I began to hear voices and commands which I thought were from God. I was overjoyed and ecstatic and thought I had found the way to God.

"I hallucinated a great deal and it was like I had entered another world. I had no concept of reality. As I obeyed the voices I heard, I lost all will of my own. I lived in this state for about a month.

"On a command from what I thought was God, I started my bedclothes on fire and sat there for a while as the blankets smoldered. When my legs started to burn, I realized what I had done and stood up to run. The blankets fell on the floor and the room burst into flames. I tried to run and couldn't move. When I opened my mouth to scream, no sound came out. That's the last thing I remember ... I was burning alive and couldn't move.

"My mother pulled me out of the burning room and I spent two months in the hospital.

"I have since been saved and baptized in the Holy Spirit. Jesus is delivering me from the subjection and oppression I was under. He is healing my memories and emotions. You are welcome to use my story."

(Name withheld by request)

After reading the letter the first thing I did was call two women I knew who were prominent members of that organization hoping that I could warn them of the

danger. Neither one seemed worried about her involvement, however, and one of them, an owner of my old
hangout cosmic bookstore, was actually insulted.

"Why, I'm a sixth-degree inititate of that organization!
I have never experienced anything so terrible. Was that
person on drugs when that happened? Our group specifically warns people not to do hallucinogens while
meditating. That kind of mixing opens the chakras to all
sorts of lower astral beings and if it weren't for guardian
angels, many more people would be in danger!"

I tried to explain that the real trap for New Agers is
that while they enter "lower" and "higher" astral levels,
the only real difference is how the "spirits" allow themselves to be portrayed. The "astral level" that all of us
had tried so hard to reach is what the Bible calls the
realm of fallen angels and they all do Satan's bidding.

"Perhaps some seekers have indeed been protected
by God's holy angels," I told her, "but the progression of
Satan's counterfeits is to treat the seeker to benevolent
'guides' until full trust is gained. Gradually, the guides
begin filling the seeker's mind with pride, then despair,
until the grotesque manifestations of these demons are
truly revealed and the seeker meets with death or psy-
chotic disorders — if he survives."

The woman on the other end of the line wasn't convinced.

"It really makes me mad," she snapped. "One person
has a 'bad trip,' blames it on an organization and gives
the whole movement a bad name."

No wonder she was upset. With negative press like
that, this woman could shortly be out of business! I
promised to find out if the victim had been using drugs
and hung up.

When I reached the person by phone, I was told that

drugs *had* been part of her early experimentation but not during this incident. In fact she had not been on drugs several months prior to turning to meditation.

It wouldn't really have mattered whether a New Ager experimented with hallucinogenic drugs along with meditation exercises since either practice has been known to produce identical effects.

Former Hindu guru Rabindranath R. Maharaj, author of *Death of a Guru: a Hindu Comes to Christ,* said in an interview for the prophetic magazine *Perhaps Today* that yoga is "dangerous." The individual begins to "meditate, to look into himself, in order to find his true self and to find that the (S)elf is God. In emptying the mind and meditating in the Eastern way, one reaches a state of passivity, and in this state I believe that demons can enter the mind and produce any amount of mystical experiences. One may see bright lights, bright colors or mystical beings. He experiences what we may call a trans-astro projection or astro journeys. I had a lot of that type of experiences, through my own yoga practices . . . I was most astonished to discover that many (of those who had been hooked on drugs) had exactly the same experiences through their drugs that I had as a Hindu through my meditation practices. I came to the conclusion that the source must be the same, namely demonic."

When I followed the teachings from Ram Dass (an American who was a Harvard graduate and worked closely with LSD promoter Timothy Leary) I read about the time when he gave megadoses of the psychedelic drug to a Hindu mystic. The mystic did not feel any changes whatsoever whereas the dosage might have caused a lesser initiate to O.D.!

None of us on the Quest expected to lean on drugs as the only method of attaining higher consciousness. They were only meant to speed up the process. The tragedy is that far too many lost their lives or their minds from an occult practice that equals mystical methods. Christian gospel singer Chuck Girard said, "Drugs are a form of sorcery which comes from the root word of pharmacy, 'pharmakeia' (magic, witchcraft) and opens people to demonic influences and possession."

A few days later a second letter came in response to my ad. It was from a young man who had experienced frightful events that also landed him in the hospital. He said that his occult practices were making him feel like he was on drugs but he hadn't been using them either.

His letter said:

"I started in the occult when I was 17. It began with two books, one about mysticism and another about achieving whatever you want by imagining what you want in your mind and telling yourself certain phrases and ideas. One night I picked up the book on achieving things, and something happened; I suddenly felt powerful. I felt like I was on drugs, but I wasn't. Demons must have come into my soul because the more I read, the more powerful I felt. I learned more and more about how to do certain things. Then I tried it out on family and friends, at school and at my job. It brought me money, popularity and success.

"The more I read the more strange I felt. Then I somehow happened across a Bible. It was like magic but completely different from the occult. I read and I felt good about reading the Bible passages. I started wondering who has control over me? I knew something was wrong. I then went into the Bible, especially Proverbs. Then trouble happened. My mom knew something was wrong.

"The next day I was admitted to the hospital where I was put on anti-depressant drugs because I was diagnosed as having mental depression. The doctors saw no improvement and gave me shock treatments. I had my Bible with me in the hospital and kept saying, 'Delight yourself in the Lord and He shall give you the desires of your heart.' I was in and out of the hospital and I had read another book on mysticism. I looked out a window and saw the sky change. There was something wrong; those demons must have been confusing me. I knew I had to break free. One night I called out and prayed the sinner's prayer to the Lord and I was born again.

"Although I was a Christian, these thoughts on mysticism remained until I learned how to get rid of these occult powers. Ever since, I've been free from the occult and I'm happily serving the Lord with victory over the devil and the occult. There has been healing in my family relationship."

Brett Ritchey

Another woman wrote of her intensive search on the Quest and what happened to her when she found the truth.

"From my last couple of years in high school and up until 1977, I had been interested in ESP, UFOs, tarot cards, ouija board, automatic writing and reincarnation.

"I suppose at that time I was searching for something real and substantial to hold on to but did not realize it at the time. I would jump into one part of the occult enthusiastically, then lose interest and go on to another aspect of the occult.

"When I finally became interested in reincarnation, I started to read a book about someone who claimed to have been the reincarnation of a well-known figure in the time of Jesus Christ. I did not have much contact with the Bible in my early life, except for a few Sunday school stories, but I kept thinking that something about what was being said in the book was not quite right. So I began to read the New Testament to see what the Bible had to say. As I read I became more interested in the life of Jesus.

"Still, I did not yet understand all that the life of Jesus meant, so I kept reading material on the occult. At about the time of Easter 1977 I decided to watch a TV movie called *Jesus of Nazareth*. It was during this movie that I finally *heard* the Gospel and knew exactly who Jesus really is. After seeing the movie, I committed my life to Christ and destroyed all of my books and paraphernalia having to do with the occult.

"I do not know if this testimony will help you with your research for your book but I thought you might like to hear it. I guess it is a chance for me to tell someone how I was turned from a life of darkness into a life of light. The Lord can even (break) through the occult to bring just one of his children home to him.

"P.S. Since becoming a Christian six years ago, God has blessed me with deliverance from agoraphobia. The Lord has provided me with a good, secure job for the past five years, with my own apartment, a new car and all of my needs have been met. I am now independent and able to provide and take care of myself."

Faith P. Mills

Another letter had personal significance to me because of its reference to Rosicrucians. Her atheist father "wisely" refused to allow his daughter to join the mystery school.

The Bible calls atheists "fools," as in Psalm 14:1, "The fool has said in his heart, There is no God."

Yet without the knowledge of any dangers in that secret order, this man was used by God to prevent a young woman from getting deeper into the snares of the enemy.

Characteristic of the parallel between rising spiritual "advancement" and declining moral and emotional behavior, this Quester hit bottom before being rescued by the Lord Jesus Christ.

"I have always wanted to share my testimony with others because there are so many young people out there still deceived by the same false mystic philosophies that I was. I wish I could warn them all.

"I grew up in a 'half-Christian' home. My mother was a devout Lutheran but my father was an equally devout atheist! As a child I attended church but I somehow missed the message that Jesus loved me or had died for me. All *I* heard was what a miserable sinner I was and how if I didn't shape up . . . It wasn't long until I decided that maybe my father was right. Maybe Christianity *was* just so much 'bunk.' And if there was a God and he was sending 99% of everybody to hell . . . I decided I didn't want anything to do with him anyway!

"My decision left a strange vacuum in my life, an inner yearning that friends and family just couldn't seem to fill. I was so idealistic that people were always letting me down. I always felt alone, even in a crowd. I felt different from everybody else, and, somehow I just never seemed to fit in.

"As I grew older I sought an answer to life's mystery by studying astrology, handwriting analysis, the ancient civilizations. I read endless books on the occult and even sought to join the Rosicrucians. My atheist father wisely refused to sign the permission slip!

"In college I continued my search unhindered. I dabbled in white witchcraft, tarot cards, palm-reading and self-hypnosis. I joined the Society of Psychical Research and tried to 'prove' reincarnation and develop my telepathic and clairvoyant 'abilities.' But I was still unsatisfied, lonely, haunted and incomplete.

"I studied Vedantism with its intellectual teachings. I read books on Buddhism, Hinduism, Taoism and Zen but nothing seemed to click. Then I happened on the 'mystic science' of Sant Mat, an offshoot of the Sikh Religion. This taught that we needed a perfect, living master who would enable us to merge into Sat Nam, the indescribable ocean of love from which he had descended.

"I wrote to the address given in the book thinking, with my luck, the master would have died and left no successor. I was wrong. The master's name was Charan Singh and he lived at the Dera Baba Jamal Sing in India.

"I was finally accepted for initiation and was given five words to meditate on which were the names of the five 'upper regions.' Now I had an 'astral copy' of the master with me at all times. I was to meditate on the words at least two hours a day, eschewing all meat and dairy products so as not to add to my 'karma.' I was promised that I would be rewarded with mystical experiences and. be able to see wondrous visions with my 'inner eye.'

"I hadn't learned enough about Christianity to see the flaws in the (Sant Mat) philosophy. Instead of the free gift of salvation I was expected to earn my way . . . with the assurance that it would take me no more than four incarnations to do so! I became helplessly enmeshed in the laws of karma and reincarnation. There was no comfort, no help in illness or tragedy. Whatever I reaped was what I had sown in another lifetime!

"There was an answer for everything, even for Jesus. He was a perfect master, too, but of course he had been master only to those he had personally initiated in his lifetime. He could do nothing for anyone now, having merged back into Sat Nam!

"The master had even written a book explaining the Gospel of John in the light of Sant Mat showing how Jesus' 'true' teachings had been so terribly distorted by Christianity! It was not until after I had become a Christian that I realized the master had stopped his analysis of Jesus with the nineteenth chapter. There was absolutely no mention made of Christ's resurrection! It didn't fit into their philosophy.

"Designed to appeal to all the young 'seekers,' Sant Mat also acknowledged the mastership of Buddha, Mohammed, Lao-tse, etc. It seemed that every great religious philosopher had been a 'perfect master.' It gave no real explanation why all their teachings had been so very different!

"But I believed all that they told me. I wanted very desperately to belong. I tried to follow the dictates, but I couldn't. I could never manage to meditate more than half an hour a day; trying to be a vegetarian with a husband who refused to give up meat made meals an endless hassle and I began to feel defeated and out of place among other disciples. I began to drift away.

"I tried every path I knew to find peace — but nothing changed. Soon the bottle became my god and I became a full-blown alcoholic.

"It is said that sometimes God lets us get in over our heads so that we will be willing to reach up to him. In my case it was true. There was no place to go but back to the God of my childhood. I realized that I had never completely stopped believing in him. I joined AA and was told to turn my life over to a 'higher power' but I still wanted nothing to do with Christ or dreaded Christianity.

"When I had my first child I realized that my 'god as I understood him' was no god I could teach to my child. In Sunday school I had memorized John 14:6: 'I am the Way, the Truth and the Life. No man comes unto the father but by me.' I began to wonder if the Bible was right, that Jesus *was* the only way.

"I even studied the Mormon Book about 'lost tribes' in America that portrayed Christ with power and glory. I went to my Bible for confirmation of the Mormon position searching the Old and New Testaments. There was no such confirmation of the Book of Mormon but there was so much that I had never seen before! I began to find the Lord.

"One night, I watched a Billy Graham crusade on television and suddenly knew in my heart that every word was true. I wept for joy and accepted Jesus Christ as my Lord and Savior.

"I am not perfect and never will be until I go to glory. But neither am I lost and lonely. Jesus loves me and I can love myself and others. I found a loving, Father-God that I can turn to for any need.

"Sometimes I regret all the years I wasted in my search and yet I feel that for me the long road was necessary. Having been down all the other paths I have come home at last. I know the futility of those other quests, and I have found my rest indeed.

Brenda Watkinson

"P.S. I have since been baptized in the Holy Spirit and God has blessed me with another son after I had been told I couldn't have any more children."

Another respondent briefly told of a gospel singer's need for the source of supernatural knowledge.

"I was raised in a Christian home since I was a child. However, I had unique gifts that were what many classify as supernatural. These supernatural gifts I would later realize are the gifts of discernment and the word of knowledge. During my early years I wanted to find out what these powers were and why they were bestowed on me. I sought for answers through the occult, mysticism and witchcraft.

"Finally the Lord got a hold of my life and revealed to me that I was seeking answers about the gifts of the Holy Spirit in Satan's spiritual realm! I know now that the occult and its supernatural feats are merely a counterfeit for the Holy Spirit. Many times now in my concerts (gospel), after I have sung, the Lord will speak to me about a certain individual whom I will minister to who is possibly in the occult. Once you have come out of it you still are perceptive in testing that spirit."

Jose Nardone

The next testimony arrived in the form of a cassette tape. I was especially eager to share it with my parents since Rosicrucians were also mentioned.

We sat at the dining room table and proceeded to listen to the testimony. Halfway through, the tape jammed twice, snarling the ribbon in several places. My father (who held to the belief that a devil is non-existent) chuckled, "I guess the devil doesn't want us to hear this!"

I tried to ignore the possibility. However, it did seem peculiar that this tape played smoothly on my own machine and other tapes belonging to dad ran just as easily on *his* recorder. Softly praying that the malfunction wouldn't persist, I tried to relax as the tape resumed.

At the end of the testimony my father leaned back in his chair and joked, "Whew! That's enough to scare the devil out of you!"

It was an expression — of course. But I touched my dad's hand lovingly and grinned, "That's the whole idea, you know!"

I later contacted the young man who sent this following testimony and learned that he has since gotten married and has lectured to other "mystic mixers."

"At fourteen years of age I used to listen to Black Sabbath albums constantly. By fifteen I'd read the Satanic Bible from cover to cover in about five hours. But I *never practiced* witchcraft, even though I felt driven to intensely study it. Until I was nineteen these interests were only a hobby. Then I began experiencing involuntary trances.

"While in the company of some girls, I tranced out and felt a compulsion to rape them, and that was the first thing that made me realize I was not in control of myself.

"Some friends introduced me to white witchcraft, the White Brotherhood and Rosicrucians; and I learned metaphysical techniques. I performed past-life regressions and hypnosis.

"Once during a nap I felt a tapping on my shoulder. When I awoke there was no one there. Settling back I felt a shove against me. This time I checked the house but I was alone. Next I felt a severe kick and I got really angry. Then I heard a voice that told me to lie down and relax, which I obeyed. In trance I left my body and entered the astral plane. I traveled to a place where I saw my friends at their own house. For the next six years this voice became my spirit guide who had identified himself as Zenamen.

"I did know a couple of Christians but they usually didn't stick around much because they kept accusing me of being in witchcraft, even though I insisted I was not. Sometimes I would practice draining energy from people or transferring energy from one person to another. It was very 'Star Wars!'

"Zenamen would always tell the truth. Whenever people asked me questions I'd always have the right answers and I quickly became a cosmic guru. Zenamen told me about the different planes of existence where we are before and after death.

"Not having been very familiar with spirit guides I bought countless books on the occult. Zenamen told me I was very unique and that I could be on a mission from God to fight evil and witchcraft from the side of light. I prepared myself and noticed that I only received power when I needed it, never if I tried to be showy. This convinced me that I was in tune with good and I had no desire to misuse this power.

"My Christian friends really started working on me but Satan was effective in keeping me away from Christ. I became annoyed with these Christians and sought other companions who shared my interests. We all heard rapping sounds, saw objects fly across the room, saw ghosts . . ."

"I actually wanted to be a professional ghost hunter and my mission would be to be a warrior against evil. Once I got into a psychic battle with a witch on an astral plane and, well, this is God's truth . . . or I should say Satan's truth which is a lie . . . one entity threw me to the ground! At 6 feet 4 inches and 230 lbs., let me tell you, I was convinced of the powerful forces!

"My friends and I used a lot of drugs but we drew the line at using a needle or taking downers. It's odd how I was so proud of that. One of my friends told me that he was no longer using drugs and that he was a born-again Christian. He tried to explain our need for a personal Savior but I just couldn't go along with it. I did, however, promise him that I would investigate the Bible. I had no intention of giving up my mission in the occult because it was, after all, a science.

"I spent two hours a day reading both testaments and the Holy Spirit began working with me. I almost made a commitment to Jesus Christ but instead I looked at the stacks and stacks of occult books on my shelves and wondered how I could tie in their mysteries with that of the Bible. For the next ten months my life was hell. My spiritual battles seemed endless.

"During another psychic battle two other friends were present. One was sort of a backslidden Christian and the other was my partner for our confrontation. This guy said he'd rather be the recipient of the spirit than to watch me go through it. (I was quite relieved!) The room was very cold; we heard breathing. Using a mystical rebuke in the language of Atlantis (so we had heard) we couldn't even get the words out of our mouths. The spirit threw us against the wall. Only our trembling Christian friend, with the Bible in his hand, was not touched.

"Months later I was invited to a Christian church with the ploy that I'd meet this really good-looking girl. Naturally I went but after meeting her, she took off. The church was packed and there were only two seats left in the place — of course right up front. As soon as we sat down my buddy was called away for an emergency. There I was alone but it seemed that the speaker, Rabindranath Maharaj (who co-authored with Dave Hunt *Death of a Guru: A Hindu Comes to Christ),* was speaking just to me. An altar call was given and I managed to raise my hand. That night I committed my life to Jesus Christ. God came to *me* ... He wanted me.

"I was so full of questions about the Lord that for three days I kept seeking fellowship with other Christians. I went home and took every last book and occult object out of my house and burned them and it took two and half hours! In weather too cold for anyone to go without sweaters or jackets, I stood outside in only a T-shirt without the slightest chill.

"Then I was baptized in the Holy Spirit. My language, which had always been vulgar and obscene, cleaned up right away. I stopped drinking, drugs and even cigarettes. My whole attitude had changed.

"Satan still tried to shake me up for a while. Once when I was sharing scriptures with a friend we both heard some snorting and grunting sounds. We looked at each other and tried to ignore the noise. I felt chills and we definitely felt a presence. The old familiar response to jump up and challenge this spirit in metaphysical ways rose me to my feet but my Lord gently reminded me to sit down. So I just lifted my hands in prayer, praising God and, without any fear at all, speaking the name of Jesus.

The presence left. I even rebuked Zenamen, that spirit which was *not* from God, and he never returned to torment me.

"I thank God for the new life He has given me through Jesus Christ.

"I pray that this testimony will help anyone who hears it."

Scott Bethel

As I collected the written testimonials from strangers who suffered as a result of their involvement in the occult, one more tragedy occurred in the life of a friend. I will call her Judy.

She was a vivacious teenager when I first met her. She loved to dance and party with her friends and wasn't much interested in religious things pertaining to her Jewish heritage or in her mother's practice of spiritualism.

A few years passed before I saw Judy again. She came over for a brief visit and complained about some of the stings of anti-Semitism she'd run into. I told her that Red and I had become born-again Christians and now we had a very strong attachment to the Children of Israel. She needn't worry that we'd become critical Gentiles? We explained that when Jesus offered salvation to non-Jews, we are "adopted" into the Jewish family, like "a wild branch grafted to the olive branch" (Rom. 11:11-24).

We played a record album of Messianic Hebrew music for her and after she left my husband worried about her. She'd been so optimistic about her new job as a bartender. The money she earned was to be for law school. We prayed that God would keep his hand on her.

Three months later we got a call from her mother.

Judy had dived into the ocean and had broken her neck. Although she escaped death when a friend pulled her out of the water, the chances that she'd ever move any part of her body below her neck were minimal. Tearfully I called a counselor for prayer at the Jewish Voice ministry in Arizona and a Spirit-filled believer prayed with me for Judy's salvation as well as a healing touch from Yeshua.

During a conversation with Judy's mother I learned that a spirit guide had told the woman years ago that her daughter would die a violent death before the age of twenty-one. Judy had just turned twenty-one when she had her accident but by the mercy of God she was alive.

Red and I drove three hundred miles to the hospital where Judy lay paralyzed from the neck down. I wondered how we could possibly minister to this dear young girl who might have understandably welcomed death rather than face life in a wheelchair. Sharing the room with Judy were two other young people, victims of broken necks. (Teens are among the highest percentage of accidents resulting in this kind of paralyzing injury). After greeting our young friend I found myself opening the subject of God with a question which I addressed to all three quadraplegics.

"Did any of you have a near-death experience during your accidents where you saw heaven or anything?" The words startled me for I hadn't planned asking this at all.

A nineteen-year-old boy named Jerry sat immobile in his wheelchair with a device called an angel brace and halo bolted to his anatomy. He was the first to answer.

"None of us did," he said, "but I know a man who nearly died from a shotgun blast to the chest, only he didn't see heaven; he saw HELL! And he said he saw the devil laughing at him!"

I had wanted to tell Judy that I didn't believe that God had caused this terrible accident but that it is Satan who "comes to rob, kill and destroy" (John 10:10) and God may *allow* it, for the Lord desires that "none should perish but that all shall come to repentance" (II Pet. 3:9). I knew God was not actually punishing this precious girl.

But Jerry spoke before I could, "Judy, God didn't cut you down like this, so don't you dare blame him. It was the devil who wanted you dead, just like he wants to kill off us young people with accidents and suicide (the two most frequent causes of death among youth today); God spared your life and mine. We can thank God we can still see, hear, taste, smell, talk and think. Just keep your eyes on Jesus, girl!"

My husband and I exchanged glances and acknowledged silently how God had appointed this young Christian as Judy's roommate and comforter. We prayed for all three patients and returned home.

Since then I found a book about occult cases called *To Loose the Chains* by Sergine Ananoudj with this passage from a believer in an evangelical church in Hanover:

"Our youngest child had been ill for nearly ten months and no one had been successful in finding the cause of this sickness. (Doctors and medicine only seemed to make the child's condition worse).

" 'The Lord must be speaking to us in this situation,' I thought. 'Yes, we could clearly see the hand of the evil one on the child. We prayed much but with no results . . . Even the believers gave up hope and said, 'Don't wear yourselves out anymore.'

"I asked God, 'Lord, what is wrong? Why this?' And the answer came. I had read an article by Modersohn that a curse was the result of a sin of witchcraft. Triumphantly, I said to myself, 'That doesn't (apply). I only had my cards read for a joke. There is no curse on us!' But God made me realize that I had not been serious enough with him and that one does not make fun of him with impunity . . .

"I cried fervently to God. Then he showed me my mistake. I told my wife, 'The child is bearing the consequences of the sin of our youth'. . . . We repented of our sins and humbled ourselves before God and the baby's condition improved." (Printed by Ewing Printing Inc., Gainsville, Fla. 1981).

When Moses announced the Ten Commandments from God to the Hebrew nation, the first law contained a warning:

"You shall not make for yourself an idol in the form of anything in heaven above nor on the earth beneath nor in the waters below. You shall not bow down to them or worship them; for I, the Lord your God, am a jealous God, punishing the children for the sins of the fathers to the third and fourth generation . . ." (Exodus 20:4,5).

My young friend Judy is the daughter of a psychic but I was also born into a third generation of spiritual bondage. This kind of oppression is often the most difficult to break free from as noted by Johanna Michaelson, author of *The Beautiful Side of Evil.* In her book she writes:

"It is a well-known fact among practicing occultists that their powers, their 'talent,' can be inherited down to the third and fourth generation. Their participation in what God has repeatedly called abomination (Deut. 18:9-14) gives Satan, the prince of this earth, the legal right to bind them and their descendants unto the third and fourth generation. Frequently, a great-grandchild will not even be aware of his ancestors' involvement until he himself, perhaps, becomes, or tries to become, a believer. Then, quite literally, all hell can break loose for him, though he himself may never have participated in occult practices. He may find it difficult to believe in Jesus, however much he may want to . . ."

Yet God has not left us without comfort. Our best weapon is still prayer. The fervent prayers of believers in behalf of the captives have led countless seekers to confront the reality of Jesus Christ. The Son of God came to redeem the children who suffer under the law and when he walked among us he showed us that through him there is healing.

"Great crowds came to Him, bringing the lame, the blind, the crippled, the dumb and others, and laid them at His feet, and He healed them. The people were amazed when they saw the dumb speaking, the crippled made well, the lame walking and the blind seeing. And they praised the God of Israel," (Matt. 15:30, 31).

God is still performing healing miracles in the name of Jesus Christ. Today Judy has the use of her hands and is planning to continue college.

The testimonies of the people I have described confirm how our Lord provided physical recoveries in addition to freedom from confusion and despair that so often accompanied our paths to "enlightenment." When we were saved we were instantly joined together in Christ and our compassion for one another magnified.

Before I became a Christian I used to mock the expression *saved*. It sounded too much like a stagnant condition of placidity, as if Christians actually believed they'd *arrived*. Anyone who was content with that position must not have desired to grow.

As a Quester I never believed that true spiritual fulfillment could occur until the transition of death into the "white light of the cosmos." Meditation and transmutation of thoughts offered glimpses of serenity but advancement was always preferable to contentedness. New Agers grope for descriptions of milestone changes of consiousness with words lke regeneration, transmutation and even dare to use the phrase born again, even though the Jesus they study is "another."

To many born-again Christians the very phrase became so over-used that they sought for more personal phrases. Catholics who once had rested on their religion and then came to a real relationship with Jesus Christ called their experience being "renewed." Protestants called it being "born from above." Former occultists who were delivered from darkness and deception call their conversion experience as having been "rescued."

We were indeed saved. But when we say rescued it is because we know just what we were rescued *from*. The evidence was materializing all over the world and in the beginning of this decade a few of us trembled at the picture that was forming.

12

Private Investigator

Throughout the years of my involvement in metaphysics and mysticism I relentlessly looked for clues to verify my purpose on the Quest. Now I was just as determined to understand how I had been so easily deceived.

I wanted to know more about the origins, goals and methods of the New Age religions and was surprised to discover even more evidence in my own personal library.

Shortly after my conversion to Christ I had taken the advice of some other believers that I clean out all occult items and books from my collection. However, I kept a few samples of New Age literature.

One day I picked up one of my old New Age magazines dated March 1978 and noticed the cover title "Special Issue: Perils of the Path." A summary of the contents read "New Age Looks at the 'New Age'" and its purpose was to warn its readers of particular dangers.

I quickly turned to the section entitled "Kundalini Casualties," which was an interview with biomedical engineer Itzhak Bentov.

In the article Bentov described some of the severe repercussions of kundalini yoga. Possible symptoms included "the left leg becoming more or less paralyzed; pseudo-heart attacks; a luminous, bluish-white light filling the head; temporary blindness; degeneration of the optic nerve; and emotionally unstable people quickly ending up in a mental hospital."

Other symptoms warned of "involuntary nodding of the head, involuntary sinuous (snakelike) movements of the body and an experience of breathing through a hole in the throat rather than through the nose."

Bentov explained that in order to rid oneself from these symptoms one should "take a shower each day — a cold one" or "run, jog, eat meat if necessary."

Another method he suggested for subduing the "coiled serpent" was to "visualize a beam of light coming out from the bottom of the spine . . . Eventually one will develop a sense of having a tail that is trailing on the ground . . ."

My brief exposure to kundalini yoga ten years before led me to the experience of the bluish-white light flashing in my brain but I had no idea of the dangers I was courting. Futhermore, the professor warned that "meditation, heavy massage (such as Rolfing) or acupuncture or even hatha yoga may trigger" the kundalini disturbances.

The article may have been intended as an alarm to the New Agers not to tamper with the "raising of the chakras" or self-realization techniques. Instead, he assures his followers, "First of all, they should realize that this is a positive development."

Perhaps the New Age reader could reconsider his choice of mystical techniques and narrow them down to so-called safer practices. I now saw that what this amounts to is "picking your poison!" My own generation had sampled so many poisons along the path yet I learned that we were certainly not the first generation to be led astray.

I read another article in the magazine entitled "The Wandervogel (They Gave Hitler Space)." It was described as "An Early New Age Movement" and was written by John De Graaf.

Prior to Nazi Germany the nation's youth followed after gurus and mystical philosophies. Similar to our own flower children of the early sixties, these German youngsters were attuned to nature, dressed peasant-style and enjoyed sexual freedom.

De Graaf quoted Stanley High, who in 1923 wrote *The Revolt of Youth* which said: "The political interests are tending to disappear, the great spiritual forces . . . are on the ascendency . . . There is an inexplicable reaction against conventional Christianity."

De Graaf explained that "German youth were ushering in the Golden Age."

These activities were taking place in the early 1920s when "occultism and all kinds of curious sects spread and prophets of the most fantastic causes found a ready response," he added. By 1929 the economy collapsed and changes were rapidly taking place.

"Hitler's talk of a mystical community, the 'Volksgemeinschaft,' appealed to the yearnings of an alienated youth and won over large numbers of the young . . ." De Graaf said.

Hitler intensified his cause to establish law and order by blaming Jews and Communists and he "appealed most to the Protestant youth groups or 'Bible circles' which abounded in Germany," De Graef said. And, by 1931 "more than 70 percent of the Bible circles members were pro-Nazi."

This magazine had once been a favorite periodical of mine but as I studied the pages more carefully I wondered how I'd missed the connection. In the short time that I attempted to blend my religion into a cosmic interpretation I had ignored the swastika on the pages of my "mystical Jesus" book.

No wonder my New Age friends had been so insistent that they too experienced revelations of the Scriptures or that they had "inside information" of the Christ. Hitler studied eastern philosophy and evidently attempted to apply it to the Bible. His goal of Aryan purity mirrored the Hinduistic caste system. The Great White Brotherhood had plans for mankind as well as for its planetary masters!

Rabindranath R. Maharaj, a former guru who now is a Christian, said in his autobiography *Death of a Guru: A Hindu Comes to Christ,* that this doctrine was "Probably devised by the Aryan founders of Hinduism in order to keep the dark-skinned Dravidians they conquered in quiet subjection . . . The doctrines of karma and reincarnation followed naturally, teaching that those of lower castes by accepting their lot in life uncomplainingly could improve their karma and thus hope for a higher reincarnation the next time around."

I shuddered at the thought of the horrible extremes emerging from this philosophy. For example, east Indians reportedly refuse to kill insects or rats which devour their grain, just as they will not use their cattle for meat.

It is against their religion.

But Americans have westernized the Hindu philosophy by claiming that humans cannot reincarnate into any life form lower than man. When I first attended Unity I watched an adult swat a spider to death and then announce, "I release you to a higher consciousness!"

Extermination of humans who were suspected of contributing to a lower consciousness became Hitler's "Final Solution." They didn't fit in with his plans for a mystical community.

The research I was accumulating had centered upon the religions apart from the Judeo-Christian faith. It was time to learn more about my roots as a born-again believer.

If I had taken a college course in world religions I might have recognized my former New Age philosophy by the descriptions of early *gnosticism*: "a belief of special knowledge of spiritual truth by faith and that matter is evil and emancipation comes through knowledge." I had been taught to deny all appearances of evil but was led to accept the idea that anything non-spiritual (and thus physical or material) was a lower vibration of energy. Aquarian doctrines pointed to dismissals of the actual events surrounding the virgin birth, the anointing of Jesus, his death upon the cross and his resurrection.

But now as I studied church history, I discovered that second century gnostics were working just as ardently to dispel the truth of the gospel.

Bruce L. Shelley described their beliefs in *Church History in Plain Language* as "what we call *dualism*, that is, they believed that the world is ultimately divided between two cosmic forces, good and evil. In line with much Greek philosophy, they identified evil with matter.

Because of this they regarded any Creator God as wicked . . . Their own Supreme Being was far removed from any such tendency to 'evil'."

Shelley explained that gnostics divided individuals into three categories: "The lower spiritual class lived by faith, the illuminated or the perfect, lived by knowledge. Still a third group, the spiritually disadvantaged, was not capable of *gnosis* under any circumstances. Some capricious deity had created them without the capacity to 'see' even under the best guru."

I remembered the times I had condescendingly excused uninterested acquaintances (who avoided my New Age suggestions) as "ignorant." I had mentally boxed those people into the same category as fundamentalist Christians who were satisfied with simple confession of salvation. Now I began to see that God had protected those dear people from deceptions. And to think I had subscribed to the platitude, "When the student is ready, the teacher will appear!"

God did not wait for students and teachers to match up. He sent the Savior.

"The Lord is not slow in keeping His promise, as some understand slowness. He is patient with you, not wanting anyone to perish, but everyone is come to repentance" (II Pet. 3:9).

The roots of my faith are grounded in the history of the Hebrew nation, set apart from pluralistic gods, and God blessed the Jews for their loyalty. Yet I had ignored the Bible for years, determined to find more "ancient" facts about my existence. The few times I did refer to the Bible I had always tried to search for deeper interpretations, just as the gnostics of the early church had done.

"Gnosticism holds an important lesson for all Christians who try to disentangle the gospel from its involvement with 'barbaric and outmoded' Jewish notions about God and history," Shelley warns. "It speaks to all who try to raise Christianity from the level of faith to a higher realm of intelligent knowledge and so increase its attractiveness to important people."

The historian was hopeful that the early gnostics were merely a part of a passing trend, for he says, "One could hardly call Gnosticism a movement; it lacked a unifying cause."

I briefly shared the sentiment that New Age religion would have to pass away as Questers continued to make their exodus from delusion into truth.

Shelley comforted that hope! "Nothing is as fleeting in history as the latest theories that flourish among the enlightened and nothing can be more easily dismissed by later generations."

In June of 1982 that hope faltered. Instead of diminishing, gnosticism was flourishing again. The words coming from the television program confirmed my suspicions. Constance Cumbey was being interviewed by Gary Randall. He introduced her as "a woman who has done extensive research on what she calls the New Age Movement."

I sat and listened incredulously as she reported her discoveries of a New Age Christ called Maitreya who was scheduled to appear to the world. She spoke of Nazism and explained that Hitler had participated in experiments with hallucinogens along with his S.S. Occult Bureau. She also quoted major leaders of the current New Age politics.

This was no passing trend. The "modern gnostics"

now openly admitted their "unifying purpose," and one of its spokespersons, Marilyn Ferguson, called it an "Aquarian Conspiracy." The New Age leaders confessed that the Movement was larger than anyone imagined.

As Constance Cumbey described the scriptural guidelines for recognizing the Antichrist, I cried softly. God had so gently opened my eyes in the privacy of a small-town environment and now he was raising up others with greater visibility to set the captives free. It was time to yank the covers off the secret and hidden things, and his promise was being fulfilled: "For there is nothing covered, that shall not be revealed; and hid, that shall not be known" (Matt. 10:26).

The names of precious friends of mine who had not wanted to listen to my warnings reminded me that I could not retreat from the work I had begun. A terrifying scenario developed in my imagination: think of all those dear seekers who would reject the warnings, only to come to the realization that the very Christ-Self master they followed was indeed the personification of the Antichrist.

Then the words of the prophets were being spoken on the television and I heard the admonition to take a stand.

"Strengthen ye the weak hands, and confirm the feeble knees. Say to them that are of a fearful heart, Be strong, fear not: Behold, your God will come with vengeance, even God with recompense; He will come and save you." (Isa. 35: 32-34).

"The people that do know their God shall be strong, and do exploits. And they that understand among the people shall instruct many . . ." (Dan. 11:32, 33).

Constance Cumbey had fit together the pieces of the

gigantic puzzle of end-times apostasy and as I stood back to examine it from a better perspective, I stepped up my own participation. The first thing I did was send for her transcripts. Wielding documented evidence, I returned to my New Age friends with greater urgency. Predictably, I wasn't well received.

Some flatly did not believe her any more than they would believe me. Others were aghast when they heard about Hitler but insisted that they weren't vulnerable to any global plot. A few accused me of attempting to ride on the coattails of a witchhunt. My parents were smitten by my seeming betrayal and even my Christian friends looked at me a little suspiciously.

After Constance Cumbey's book, *The Hidden Dangers of the Rainbow* was released I had the opportunity to meet her in Florida. Red and I listened to her speak to a congregation of believers who may not have known much about New Age but they knew about the Bible's prophecies. Several people were noticeably shaken with the realizations and during the altar call adults and young children came forward to give their lives to Jesus Christ.

Red squeezed my hand and whispered, "I'm really glad we heard Connie in person. Her heart is for souls. I'm convinced that she is not just trying to tear down people's character or using scare tactics. She's on to something real."

We enjoyed our time with her and I was relieved to hear her testimonies of people who had come out of the movement as a result of her warnings. I prayed that God would deliver my own loved ones from spiritual bondage very soon.

I have heard that God answers prayers three ways: "Yes, no, and not now." It has been a gradual process for some of my friends and family, as these have been attempting to sort out the chaff from the wheat. It took them many years to approach God intellectually; their descent to humility, admitting they'd been as deceived as I had been, has been slow but certain.

Sunny confessed that "full-moon mediations belong to pagan rituals" and she has begun to understand why her "cosmic plays and 'third testament' haven't succeeded after all these years."

My parents have studied the documented evidence and I have watched with joyful expectancy while they compared their books to the Bible.

Jody also had some news to tell me. She had read *The Hidden Dangers of the Rainbow* and examined the clippings and letters I sent to her. Her ultimate confrontation occurred when she visited her guru, the Scottish "seer."

"I laid it all out in black and white," Jody told me. "I had to know what she thought about the claims that this was the religion of the Antichrist."

For a moment I cringed. I hardly expected Jody's guru to admit to any such conspiracy. Instead, the seer apparently was pleased at Jody's perception.

"She told me that it was all exactly correct," my friend sighed. "That really pulled the plug out for me. I practically feel like an agnostic now."

I explained to Jody that if she understood the meaning of *agnostic* as one who is non-committal toward religion or believes that "the existence of God is unknown and probably unknowable" at least now she would understand how she and I had been *gnostics*. Our former beliefs included the acceptance of heavenly messengers commuting back and forth from God to man, and we were wide open for deceptive influences.

I sensed her hopelessness on the other end of the phone and heard her say, "I guess I feel like all I want to think about is, 'Well, God, it's just you and me.'"

Recalling a similar position of helplessness not so long ago, silently I rejoiced for my friend — she was experiencing the brokenness of submitting to God.

"Jody, that's a beautiful place to be," I assured her. "Now you can be filled with God's own restoration."

After our conversation I thought about how painful it is to have to confront loved ones with unwelcome exhortation. It is no less painful to receive. Like the parental promise that accompanies chastisement, "This hurts me more than it hurts you," the recipient doesn't quite believe that's possible. But our friendship survived and through the blood of Jesus Christ we can be much more than "soul sisters." With the adoption by our Father, we can be true sisters in Christ.

The Holy Spirit has moved mightily in preparing my loved ones. He has pierced through the enemy's fortress with the sword of truth, in spite of the tactics hurled at the captives to prevent them from leaving Satan's camp. Leaders in the New Age Movement have carefully taught their followers to avoid anyone or anything that sounds "negative, critical, judgmatic, fearful or narrowminded."

Yet Jesus preached that there is only one way to the Father, through the Son. Dave Hunt presented an excellent picture for those who argue that the Bible is "narrow-minded dogmatism," or "too simplistic."

"The gospel declares that the only remedy is to give ourselves to Jesus Christ, believing that he died for our sins and rose again, to invite him to come into and cleanse our hearts." (Those who reject this "narrow-minded remedy") "would be stunned if, after being examined by a doctor for a serious problem and asking for the results, the doctor replied: 'I'm not so narrow-minded and dogmatic as to come up with a *definite* diagnosis, I would not want to push *my truth* on you. What would you like? Open-heart surgery has been popular lately or I could transplant a kidney. I believe that every person is entitled to the operation of his choice.' No one denies that this is absurd. Yet when it comes to diagnosing society and establishing a basis for eternal destiny through a right relationship with God, suddenly everyone gets 'broad-minded' and insists that God. . . should go along with whatever we choose, as long as we are 'sincere' about it,'' Hunt wrote.

And so the New Age leaders painstakingly practice outstanding sincerity and all-embracing love as an example to their followers "not to listen to the critical." Their sincerity and overflowing love are undoubtedly their best virtue and is something from which all of us could learn a lesson. However, as they attempt to merge gnosticism, psychic practices and occult beliefs with Christianity, the leaders fervently admonish the gullible to steer clear of arguments.

One of these leaders is Elizabeth Clare Prophet, the spokesperson for Summit Lighthouse or Church Universal and Triumphant. After I met with Constance Cumbey I happened to see Ms. Prophet's program on cable television. It was titled "The Everlasting Gospel," featuring "The True Teaching of Jesus Christ."

When I first heard the opening strains of *Amazing Grace* being sung by her congregation, I hoped that this woman had gotten saved and was no longer preaching apostasy. However this disciple of Maitreya and St. Germain and other "ascended masters" had only included Jesus in the string of avatars.

Ms. Prophet quoted from the Beatitudes and then talked about karma. She preached about "the Buddha we are about to become" and explained that the ritual of water baptism was a symbol of the "Divine Mother."

She herself is described in the Summit's brochure as "representative of the World Mother" who calls the enlightened into "the Coming Revolution in Higher Consciousness." Her mission is called "the Great Synthesis of the Mother Flame."

The blending of mysticism and Christianity, or synthesis (a bringing together of many parts to form a whole) results in synthetic religion. *Synthetic* is defined as "not genuine" and is a perfect synonym for "counterfeit." It is no accident that Satan is busy counterfeiting the gifts of the Holy Spirit more intensely.

Ms. Prophet warned her congregation to "stay away from churches who do not preach the Holy Spirit." She referred to mainline churches as "cold, stagnant and partakers of the Antichrist." Instead, cosmic "Christians" were encouraged to attend charismatic churches where they would be welcome and comfortable!

I shared these statements with a born-again, Spirit-filled Christian woman, Darline More, who was born into a seventh-generation of Satan worshipers before coming to Christ. She told me that before she ever renounced witchcraft she attended a charismatic church for months, not even knowing that there was any difference between the religions!

Since then, she underwent deliverance from demonic influences and she now immerses herself in the Word of God. But she is equally alarmed at the acceptance of psychic activities unknowingly being allowed in both charismatic and mainline churches. Her town's local Methodist church advertised an expert's demonstration of levitation! My friend often warned church members to "test the spirits" or "weed out occult influences." (Frequently former occultists who have truly renounced psychic activities are more equipped to discern the masquerading angels of light). However, many times Christian brothers and sisters told her she was paranoid, or immature, or perhaps in need of "more deliverance." This is a familiar refrain to those who recognize Christian teaching which borrows from mind-control tactics.

Johanna Michaelsen formerly practiced Silva Mind Control and psychic surgery. She makes no apologies for being a charismatic believer, but joins in the cautious appeal to discern the gifts.

"For example, believers with occultic backgrounds which have never been renounced are manifesting mediumistic gifts and techniques which go undiscerned in the atmosphere of the ecstatic hoopla which frequently characterizes so many meetings. Some of these believers are often still involved in such things as astrology and palm reading, and usually completely unaware of the spiritual dangers involved," she writes.

Jesus warned us of false prophets *"which come to you in sheeps clothing, but inwardly they are ravening wolves. Ye shall know them by their fruits. Do men gather grapes of thorns, or figs of thistles? Even so every good tree brings forth good fruit; but a corrupt tree brings forth evil fruit. A good tree cannot bring forth evil fruit, neither can a corrupt tree bring forth good fruit," (Matt. 7:15-18).*

God is still allowing the wheat and the tares to grow together until the time of harvest. And harvest time is nearer than ever. This decade has produced throngs of individuals who inspected their own denominations *and* cults in order to ascertain whether their pet doctrines truly agree with the scriptures.

The Holy Spirit, whom Jesus promised would guide unto all truth, assists believers in this "fruit inspection" by always confirming agreement of the Bible. As a result, disciples of Jesus Christ are "coming out from among" the mystery teaching of "Babylon" (See Rev. 18:1-4).

One of the very first Christians that God brought to me when I attempted to blend mysticism with Christianity gave me a basic understanding of "fruits," when she said, "Trying to mix two together creates a hybrid, and a hybrid plant doesn't reproduce. It's the same thing with a horse and a donkey. You get a stubborn mule."

I had been one of those stubborn mules who didn't want to listen to reason or to the truth of the Gospel.

I want to be one of my Master's trusting sheep, that I may hear his voice. Before I met the Good Shepherd I tried to follow after strangers who were themselves led astray like lost sheep.

"He who enters by the door is the shepherd of the sheep. To him the gatekeeper opens; the sheep hear this voice, and he calls his own sheep by name, and leads them out. When he has brought out all his own, he goes before them, and the sheep follow him, for they know his voice. A stranger they will not follow, but they will flee from him, for they do not know the voice of strangers . . . I am the door of the sheep . . . if anyone enters by me, he will be saved, and will go in and out and find pasture. . . I know my own and my own know me, as the Father knows me and I know the Father; and I lay down my life for the sheep," (John 10:1 15).

"Behold, I stand at the door and knock; if any one hears my voice and opens the door, I will come in . . ." (Rev. 3:20).

13

Forum: New Agers'
Dilemmas — and Comments

As Christians and New Agers peer across the gulf of opposing religious beliefs, they have specific topics that remain puzzling. I have been asked frequently to address these subjects and many of them were problems that I, too, had once addressed.

I do not pretend to be an authority. I sought viewpoints from Christian sources as well as from among New Age references. My Bible was my ever present guide.

If you are a New Ager or a "cosmic Christian" trying to sort out your beliefs, I pray that this forum will assist you in the sifting process.

As a Christian, perhaps it will aid you for more effectively witnessing to those cults and the occult. As most "occult investigators" will testify, it is not recommended that anyone attempt to delve into the darkness just for curiosity or information. Better to know the Word of God intimately than to concentrate on all the counterfeits.

May God receive all the glory for your "getaway" from the deceiver and remember the words of Dave Edwards in his poem "The Getaway:" (c. 1981, Half Circle Bud/ Dayspring, used by permission.)

> *"In the moonlight you would trip me,*
>   *try to fool me in the night,*
> *For the darkness keeps your secrets well enough.*
> *But I'll know your imperfections when I see you*
>   *in the Light,*
> *And you'll never catch me falling for your bluff.*
>
> *You have shown me things that others*
>   *find impossible to see,*
> *How your beauty's just a certain side you show.*
> *You're as lovely as a spectre,*
>   *now you've shown yourself to me,*
> *You are everywhere but no one seems to know."*

Here are the New Age puzzles and my comments:

Dilemma:

If only people would understand that the Aquarian religion is *not occult!* We are completely removed from psychism. Ours is a study of science and of ancient wisdom.

Comment:

"Occult" is defined as "secret, mysterious, concealed, relating to supernatural agencies, their effects, and knowledge of them" (Webster's Collegiate Dictionary).

Black witchcraft practices are opposite to God's Truth, but mysticism belongs to the "grey occult." Blending

certain biblical principles with secret teachings is the
subtle pollution of God's revealed truth.

*"For the time is coming when people will not endure
sound teaching, but having itching ears they will accumu-
late for themselves teachers to suit their own likings, and
will turn away from listening to the truth and wander into
myths"* (II Tim. 4:3-5).

Dilemma:

But I love the Bible! Jesus has shown us that love will
conquer and uplift man. As we approach the coming of
the Kingdom we rejoice that Jesus has enlightened us to
understand the messages he gives those who seek him.

Comment:

In a chapter entitled "New Gospels for a New Age,"
several messages were given to James Padgett in 1915
through automatic writing. He called a second volume
True Gospel Revealed Anew by Jesus. Then he received
"1500 such messages upon many subjects, but mostly as
to things ... unorthodox, and as to the errancy of the
Bible." A chapter subtitle reads "The Power of Love to
Redeem Men from Sin and Error." The "messages from
Jesus" address this Love and say "It changes not, nor is
it ever bestowed on anyone who is unworthy, or refuses
to seek for it in the only way provided by the Father,"
(*Revelation: The Divine Fire* by Brad Steiger, Berkeley
Books, N.Y., 1973, 1981).

The message of the true gospel is that of grace, bestowed upon the unworthy and given to those who seek
diligently. But *"if someone comes and preaches another
Jesus than the one we preached, or if you receive a different spirit from the one you received, or if you accept a
different gospel from the one you accepted, you submit to*

it readily enough," (II Cor. 11:4).

"Why do you not understand what I say? It is because you cannot bear to hear my word. You are of your father the devil, and your will is to do your father's desires. He was a murderer from the beginning, and has nothing to do with truth, because there is not truth in him. When he lies, he speaks according to his own nature, for he is a liar and the father of lies" (John 8:43, 44).

"Jesus Christ is the same yesterday and today and forever. Do not be led away by diverse and strange teachings . . ." (Hebrews 13:8, 9).

Dilemma:

The devil is just a scapegoat for man's own failings. Man's negativity has produced the ills of this world. When he purifies his thoughts in love, we shall see a perfect world.

Comment:

That is exactly what the writer of *The Ultimate Frontier* said when he wrote ". . . your environment is the result of your own thoughts and actions. You, and you alone, are responsible for everything you enjoy and suffer in this life," (page 120). This is also the same book which advised seekers to stay away from churches because they are part of the Antichrist! When my Christian friend, the ex-Satanist, saw this book she pointed out that the teachings it contained were identical to those accepted by devil-worshippers!

God's Word describes the spirit of the real Antichrist as one who will endeavor to set up a religion based upon man, and six is his number. Lucifer was thrown out of heaven for attempting to ascend to God's throne. If Satan can tempt man to follow the same plan, he will do everything he can to achieve his original goal.

Dilemma:
Well, I certainly know the difference between God's messengers and demonic spirits. I have no fear of being influenced by wicked entities.

Comment:
Satan is also clever. He knows that if he can't scare you or seduce you with obvious tactics, he will send "beautiful and loving" emissaries to lure the seeker into deception.

"And no wonder, for Satan himself masquerades as an angel of light. It is not surprising, then, if his servants masquerade as servants of righteousness" (II Corinthians 11:14).

Dilemma:
Fear is the opposite of faith. I will not listen to any teachings that are based upon fear.

Comment:
And so, like an ostrich, you pretend that if you don't confront the words which cause fear and trembling, they will all go away. I never met a New Ager who wasn't afraid of something, whether it was fear of poverty, poor health, commitments or world conditions. Yet when I was finally confronted with the Word of God, I trembled with fear. This fear, or intense awe of Almighty God *"is the beginning of knowledge; fools despise wisdom and instruction"* (Proverbs 1:7).

It may take courage to face the words of admonition

but the New Age dropouts I've met all confessed their gratitude for God's awesome instruction.

Once we have surrendered to Jesus Christ we can trust him to deliver us from ungrounded fears, *"For God did not give us a spirit of timidity but of power and love and self-control" (II Tim. 1:7).*

Dilemma:

How could there be anything wrong with having a psychic healer alleviate pain or illness for a person? I think that if somebody took away my pain, I'd say "Thank you!" no matter what he was into!

Comment:

Johanna Michaelsen spent a great deal of time working closely with "psychic surgeons" and assisted in over 200 such supernatural "healings." All along she assumed these powers were from God, until events caused her to question the source. Just because an individual has a power to heal or to speak in unknown languages is not a sign that God is with him. Johanna Michaelson says, "One of the ways occultic powers are transferred from a spiritist or witch to someone else is through the laying on of hands" (page 186).

Dilemma:

Then are all gifts of the supernatural evidence of satanic influence?

Comment:

Before there could be a counterfeit there had to be an original. Satan works hard to copy the miracles of God. It would only give him more power if he could get all

Christians so fearful of the *charisms* that they dis-
continued believing in the power of the Lord God. The
Bible reminds us to "test the spirits," to discern the
fruits of believers.

When Christians defend their "revelations" by their
"feelings" or insist that what they have experienced is
real, there could be a lack of discernment and scriptural
foundation.

Dilemma:

There must be a reason for why I have been given an
understanding for esoteric knowledge. God will give me
a sign if I'm not supposed to follow this path.

Comment:

As a former New Ager I, too, was looking for a reason
behind every little event and sought signs from God for
my direction. Each time I sincerely believed that God
had been guiding me and that the "clues" along the path
were signs from God. I continually affirmed "all things
work together for good." I wasn't aware that I was only
partially quoting the Bible.

*"And we know that all things work together for good to
them that love God, to them who are called according to
His purpose" (Rom. 8:28).*

*"An evil and adulterous generation seeks for a sign; but
no sign shall be given to it except the sign of the prophet
Jonah. For as Jonah was three days (and nights) in the
belly of the whale, so shall the Son of man be three days
(and nights) in the heart of the earth" (Matt. 12:39).*

Jesus promised that signs would follow after believers

(see Mark 16:17) and that prior to his return great signs in the heavens will appear (Matt. 24:24).

These days I am not preoccupied with "how" and "why;" I rejoice that one day all my questions will be answered when I meet him face to face (I Cor. 13:12).

Dilemma:

How do you explain the driving thirst for knowledge or wisdom that bonds New Agers?

Comment:

I say we've all been homesick for heaven and when mundane matters of life appear lackluster, our souls, longing for paradise, are compelled to seek heavenly things. Sadly, our search led us to glittering streets of fool's gold!

"It is to be observed that God has never, since the fall of man, revealed anything to gratify a mere thirst for knowledge," writes G.H. Pember in *Earth's Earliest Ages*. For "knowledge in this life is a gift fraught with peril: for our great task here is to learn the lesson of the absolute dependence upon God, and entire submission to His will. . . but knowledge, unless it be accompanied by a mighty outpouring of grace, causes undue elation. . ."

Dilemma:

I don't see any harm in reading my horoscope. Astrology can be a game.

Comment:

Astrology is a religion; it is occult in origin. Once you have accepted Jesus Christ you have no need to consult the stars or planets.

"Formerly, when you did not know God, you were slaves to those who by nature are not gods. But now that you know God — or rather are known by God — how is it that you are turning back to those weak and miserable principles? Do you wish to be enslaved by them all over again? You are observing special days and months and seasons and years! I fear for you, that somehow I have wasted my efforts on you." (Gal. 4:11).

My friend Gladys likes to say, "I *used* to be a Leo; when I was born again my sign became the sign of the cross."

Dilemma:

Why would you want to associate yourself with a symbol of execution! The cross was just the method used in Jesus' day for the death penalty. It would be like wearing a replica of an electric chair today!

Comment:

The early church of Catholicism portrayed the suffering Jesus on all crucifixes. Today several charismatic churches have designed the Catholic cross with Jesus risen and triumphant over death. Other crosses remain without the body of Christ to signify that he has ascended to the Father, but the cross is a reminder of the penalty Jesus paid for our redemption.

I grew up attending a church which had no cross at all. Our goal was to achieve our own Christed being. The substitutionary death of Jesus was "crossed out" until none of us remembered the suffering of the precious Saviour. This is precisely what the adversary seeks to do: blot out the memory of Christ's provision of man's reconciliation to God.

Dilemma:

All this talk about blood. I've never understood why it is brought up all the time. Isn't it only a spiritual symbol?

Comment:

God established covenants that required blood sacrifices for the atonement of sins. (A practice common among pagan cultures, also). Every year the high priest entered the Holy Tabernacle with blood offerings for the sins of the people using blood of perfect lambs, doves, etc.

"In fact, the law requires that nearly everything be cleansed with blood; and without the shedding of blood there is no forgiveness" (Heb. 9:22).

When John the Baptist saw Jesus approaching he announced, "Behold, the Lamb of God, which taketh away the sin of the world" (John 1:19). Jesus offered himself pure and spotless as the sacrifice for all of us.

Believers are aware of the costly grace and mercy provided for them and they offer praise "unto him that loved us, and washed us from our sins in his own blood, and hath made us kings and priests unto God and His father ..." (Rev. 1:5).

The celebration of Passover signifies God's protection for his children held captive in Egypt. The blood of lambs upon the doorpost covered them over. The new Passover, given at the Lord's last supper, signifies his shed blood as our covering. Jews who have accepted Jesus as Messiah often celebrate both.

Dilemma:

What about all the myths and legends and ancient religions? I studied so many of them; how could I have been so off-base? I really do love God!

Comment:

St. Augustine is quoted to have said, "God places salt on our tongues so that we might thirst for Him." Seeds of truth have been planted over the ages and the myth became fact in Jesus Christ.

God knows our hearts. If you have been sincerely seeking his truth God will lead you to a place where you *can* choose him. "No one can come to me unless the Father who sent me draws him; and . . . it is written 'they shall all be taught by God.' Everyone who has heard and learned from the Father comes to me" (John 6:44).

Dilemma:

It is superstitious to believe in a devil or demons. I believe there is one God who is love. If I believe in a devil then I am believing in two powers, or a power other than God.

Comment:

Ah, yes. One of my old favorite rebuttals. James said it wasn't good enough just to believe in God. "Thou believest that there is one God; thou doest well: the devils also believe, and tremble" (James 2:19). Your belief or disbelief in a devil or demons doesn't affect the devil's existence. It was the best ploy Lucifer had going for him to get the "modern" world to stop believing he was real. Yet the account of Lucifer's fall from heaven, which Jesus recalled saying, "I saw Satan fall like lightning from heaven" in Luke 10:18, is recorded in Isaiah 14:13-15. Lucifer was a created being, just as the angels. His big mistake was in his conceit to exalt himself above God. Satan is not a "fragment" of God, but is the real prince of this world and organizer of Babylon, a term used for blasphemous religions.

Dilemma:

Perhaps it is possible that there are just negative emotions that affect some people, and not actual demons. I want nothing to do with negative attitudes.

Comment:

That's a noble concept, but who has ever managed an entire day without one negative emotion creeping in?

When Peter suggested to Jesus that his master flee from the guards coming to arrest him, did Jesus say, "Now, Peter, this is just a negative thought that would prevent my mission." NO! He rebuked his disciple and said, "Who gave you this idea, Peter? Satan?" and told Satan to get thee hence! (Matt. 16:23). Remember, Peter was one of Christ's closest men with whom he shared the most intimate conversations.

Dilemma:

Didn't Jesus discourage our worship of him, but only God?

Comment:

From the Scofield Reference Bible (1909-45) several scriptures are listed where Jesus affirmed his deity:

1. He applied to himself the Jehovistic I am. The Jews correctly understood this to be our Lord's claim to full deity.

2. He claimed to be Adonai of the Old Testament (Matt. 22:42-45).

3. He asserted his identity with the Father (Matt. 28:19, Mark 14:62, John 10:30).

4. He exercised the chief prerogative of God (Mark 2:5-7, Luke 7:48-50).

5. He asserted omnipresence (Matt. 18:20, John 3:13); omnipotence (Matt. 28:18, Luke 7:14, John 5:21-23, 6:19); mastery over nature and creative power (Luke 9:16-17, John 2:9, 10:28).

6. He received and approved human worship (Matt. 14:33, 28:9, John 20:28-29).

Dilemma:

The more spiritual we become we will perceive the necessity to abstain from meats. The Bible even says that in Genesis 1:29, 30: ". . . I have given you every herb bearing seed . . . for you it shall be as meat."

Comment:

God did indeed say this to Adam. The Lord established a covenant with Adam, and God has established several covenants with man which later included meats of particular varieties, in order to set apart his people called by his name. (Most people assume that these dietary laws were based solely on health reasons, although the laws probably do make good sense). We have been given seven covenants from Adam to Christ: Edenic, Adamic, Noahic, Abrahamic, Mosaic, Palestinian and Davidic. With Jesus Christ we have another covenant, simply called NEW COVENANT (Heb. 8:8-13). See the Scofield Reference Bible for definitions of the covenants.

In Timothy 4:1-3 the Word foretells signs of the latter times apostasy where some will depart from the faith and listen to seducing spirits and doctrines of devils, and they will promote celibacy and to abstain from meats. In Romans 14:13-23 the Christian is told not to make an issue over who eats meat or what kinds of meat or no meat. Other references on meat, food and drink include: Matt. 6:25. Acts 10:9-16, Matt. 15:11-18.

Our Lord in his resurrected body sat down with his disciples and enjoyed a brunch of broiled fish; had his men been shepherds, he might have dined on lamb. Christ was in his purest form and he saw fit to eat the catch of the day!

You don't have to eat meat if you don't want to, but your vegetarian diet doesn't affect your spirituality, as much as the religion of the Antichrist would have you believe. With all the junk most of us eat I am grateful for Jesus' promise of signs that will accompany believers, ". . . and if they (consume) any deadly thing, it will not hurt them!" (Mark 16:18).

Dilemma:

What's all the raising of hands and shouting amens and hallelujahs about? I'm more dignified than that. I need to worship God without all that embarrassing movement and sound.

Comment:

As I recall, there are many awkward positions required in the practice of yoga. And chanting mantras or vowel sounds while standing on your head isn't exactly "dignified."

"But when ye pray, use not vain repetitions, as the heathen do: for they think that they shall be heard for their (many words)" (Matt. 6:7). Hearty amens are responses of agreement.

"We may add that while the disciplines practiced in the Eastern religions begin with the learning of bodily posture in order thereby to foster prayer, in the charismatic movement the Spirit leads and the body follows." (Rene Laurentin, *Catholic Pentacostalism,* Doubleday & Co. Inc. 1977).

Dilemma:

You said you knew a person who almost died from the advice of a holistic doctor. I have always had more faith in preventative practices than in medical doctors who only try to treat the symptoms, not the causes.

Comments:

Me, too! But there are fine doctors in both fields. I take vitamins and try to eat healthy foods, and a good chiropractor has straightened me out more than once when I was in knots. However, even though I would not say that all holistic centers should be written off, they attract followers and even practitioners who swear to false doctrines. Interview some for yourself; as a Christian, it could turn out to be quite a field for witnessing.

Dilemma:

When you were a New Ager, you said that you always noticed a pattern of "something gained, something lost." Has that changed since you've been a Christian?

Comment:

Actually, I've noticed a reversal. The saying that things are darkest before the dawn is a close description. One Christian friend pointed out, "Whenever God is about to do something big, the enemy throws his worst obstacles at us to get us to give up!" Instead of "rebuking every troublesome situation," I have been practicing more patience — usually the Lord is about to move mightily.

Dilemma:

We shouldn't be looking for a kingdom of God to be in a certain place; Jesus said it is within you.

Comment:

In an effort to find this "inner kingdom" too often the seeker tries to bypass the entrance and creates his own "door." It is through Jesus who gives us that entrance. "He who does not enter the sheepfold by the door but climbs in by another way, that man is a thief and a robber; but he who enters by the door is the shepherd of the sheep. To him the gatekeeper opens . . ." (John 10:1).

Referring to Luke 17:21, the Scofield Reference Bible explains this passage of the kingdom. "(It) is different from the kingdom of heaven," and "would not come with observation but in the hearts of men." The kingdom of God is entered by being born again: the kingdom of heaven is "an earthly sphere of the universal kingdom of God" and "the two have almost all things in common" (page 1003).

Establishing the kingdom on earth had been the hope of the Jews who expected Messiah to reign and rule in the tradition of King David, and they renounced Jesus for his refusal to take authority militarily. Establishing a utopian kingdom on earth before Christ returns is a dangerous goal even for Christians, for Satan has been preparing the Aquarian conspirators to do just that through man's own spiritual "evolvement."

Dilemma:

I seriously doubt that Jesus' body ascended literally through the air. And this idea about a "rapture" whisking us into heaven is absurd. Our rescue from planet earth will be by space ships. The planetary brotherhood is preparing our escape.

Comment:

You can sing "Swing Low, Sweet UFO" if you want to. I prefer to wait upon the Lord God who is in the miracle business.

In their book *Encounters With UFO'S* John Weldon and Zola Levitt quoted the following from a 400-page report prefaced by Lynn E. Catoe:

"A large part of the available UFO literature is closely linked with mysticism and the metaphysical. It deals with subjects like mental telepathy, automatic writing, and invisible entities . . .

"Many of the UFO reports . . . recount alleged incidents that are strikingly similar to demoniac possession and psychic phenomena which has long been known to theologians and parapsychologists" (Harvest House Publishers, 1975, page 101).

I have personally known individuals who really thought they were so spiritually purified that all they had to do was go into the woods and just ascend!

Jesus said, "*No one has ascended into heaven but he who descended from heaven, the son of man . . .*" (John 3:13).

Dilemma:

There is no need for Jesus to return in the way people

are expecting. When we have the Christ-within, we needn't look up to the sky for him.

Comment:

At the Lord's ascension the attending angels assured the gaping disciples, *"This Jesus who was taken up from you into heaven, will come in the same way as you saw him go into heaven" (Acts 1:11).*

Jesus warned us to beware of the false prophets who say "he is here or there" (See Matt. 24:23-27). Especially watch out for those who predict an exact time or place. This is the only answer which Jesus admitted not to know himself, "but the Father only" (verse 36).

Dilemma:

What if some of the mystical prophecies do come true? Suppose Atlantis rises? Would fundamentalists try to deny the facts?

Comment:

If evidence proved that the "cosmic masters" accurately predicted signs of the Aquarian Age, no doubt New Agers would indeed celebrate a victory.

Jesus warned us that ". . . false prophets will arise and show great wonders, so as to lead astray, if possible, even the elect" (Matt. 24:24).

When the Antichrist is revealed those who "received not the love of the truth, that they might be saved" may witness powerful signs. "And for this cause God shall send them strong delusion, that they should believe a lie . . ." (II Thess. 2:10, 11).

Dilemma:

I've been told that Pegasus, unicorns and other

symbols are codes for New Age. But I don't know why we should refrain from using the rainbow! That was one of God's own creations!

Comment:

The rainbow was given as a reminder of the Creator's everlasting covenant that he would never again cleanse the earth with water. (So much for wondering when our coastlines will disappear!) However, the rainbow in cosmic circles lends to "color therapy" and signifies the link between the over-soul and man. Christians who desire to decorate their homes, cars, etc. with rainbows might consider using them in conjunction with a cross or a dove, or the name of Jesus.

Incidentally, a unicorn (Zondervan's New Compact Bible Dictionary points out) was probably a name given to an untamable ox.

Seen in profile it appeared to have but a single horn, hence the name "unicorn," (page 44).

Dilemma:

Introduction: "Hello, my name is (John Doe) but my spiritual name is (fill in the blank)."

Comment:

Perhaps your parents didn't bestow upon you a mysterious name. So you search for one that designates a cosmic connotation. If you simply cannot stand your given name, there is no reason why you can't choose to change it. But don't get fooled into thinking that it shows how spiritual you are or that it was your name in a previous life. God loves you and knows all about you. You are special enough to him without you trying to make yourself feel special with names from "other galaxies!"

Dilemma:

All of us just have different concepts of God. Our expression of wanting to become one with creation is our way of becoming one with God.

Comment:

Whose god? If you really research the religions of New Age you will find that they are based on Hinduism or Buddhism or an attempt to blend these with the Christian faith. They are not monotheistic but pluralistic, as in the dual nature of the "light and dark side of God." This is not the Creator, God of Abraham and Lord of Israel, and not the Father Jesus came to announce.

If you insist on clinging to beliefs that have nothing to do with the biblical author of life, all I can ask you is not to refer to him as the same God that you worship. At least then we can agree that your religion works for you. I renounced that religion when I accepted the Messiah.

"Ye shall not go after other gods, or the gods of the people which are round about you . . ." (Deut. 6:14).

"For though there be that are called gods, whether in heaven or in earth, (as there be gods many, and lords many) but to us there is but one God, the Father, of whom are all things, and we in him; and one Lord Jesus Christ, by whom are all things, and we by him" (I Cor. 8:5, 6).

Dilemma:

What about the reference to "wheel of birth" in the Revised Standard Version of James 3:6? Isn't this the mandala, the symbolic cycle of reincarnation? Didn't most cultures believe in reincarnation until the fifth

century when the Council of Constantinople threw out
this belief while compiling the Bible?

Comment:

That reference is also called cycle of nature. "In the
world in which Christianity arose, most of the first-
century Greek mystery religions, such as Gnosticism,
held to various theories of Karmic transmigration with
its doctrine of Christ's substitutionary atonement in
which he paid all of our 'Karmic debt' through his own
suffering. He had no karma of his own, but he suffered
and died for our sins," *The Origin of Paul's Religion*,
Wm. B. Eerdman, Pub. Co. 1965, author, Dr. Machen.

Dilemma:

The Aquarian Age is symbolized by the zodiac sign of
the "water bearer." There is a scripture that gives this as a
sign to this age in Mark 14:13.

Comment:

This was only meant as a landmark sign to the disciples who had to meet privately with their Master for
the Passover. The "man carrying a pitcher" signified the
location for their meeting; anything beyond that is
speculation.

Dilemma:

Jesus often said things that referred to "this age and
the age to come." Maybe we New Agers are right when
we calculate the Piscean, Arian and Aquarian ages, and
Jesus knew about them.

Comment:

In some translations of the Bible the term "age" is

interchangeable with "world." Historical periods in the Bible are sometimes sectioned into dispensations. New Age doctrines have charted time periods by the Zodiac, and according to one mystery schoolmaster, Eklal Kueshana, 1953 was the "date for the closing of the Piscean Age and the beginning of the Aquarian Age. An age is one-twelfth the peiod of time required by our earth to make a complete circuit of its precessional wobble, which takes about 26,000 years; so 2100 years is generally assumed the duration of an Age," *The Ultimate Frontier,* pages 60 and 61). Then he attributes the events of the Aquarian age to the revelations of St. John the Divine, "which includes the last half of this century."

When Jesus took his turn to read from the scrolls in the synagogue, "He opened the book and found the place where it is was written" (in Isaiah 61:1, 2) that the Spirit of the Lord had sent him "to proclaim the acceptable year of the Lord's favor," but Christ stopped before the passage "and the day of vengeance of our God."

Dilemma:
What about the missing years of Christ? Other cultures refer to having seen Jesus.

Comment:
Extensive though controversial accounts of this period abound. One is a documentary film by Aura Productions called *The Lost Years of Christ.* Texts found at Nag Hammadi in Egypt in 1948 were discovered and reportedly written by other disciples, called "The Gnostic Gospels." Speculation over the allusion to these travels are pounced upon by esoteric seekers when they

recite John, "there are also many other things which Jesus did, were every one of them to be written, I suppose that the world itself could not contain the books that could be written" (closing statement of the gospel of John).

Those "missing years" are described in the *Aquarian Gospel*, and copies of this book are frequently stocked in Unity bookstores. However, one of Unity's own teachers, Herbert J. Hunt, expressed his doubts of the validity. He says in *A Study of the New Testament* that "Luke (who tells us that he made careful inquiries concerning all the activities of Jesus) certainly would have given additional emphasis to Luke's theme: Jesus, Saviour of mankind ... Moreover, Jesus himself rejected all suggestions regarding outside influences upon his teaching. He claimed that his knowledge came direct from the Father ... People spoke of Jesus not as the 'great traveler' but as the Man from Nazareth."

Dilemma:

Christianity is supposed to be so full of love for one another. How can Christians tell people who have believed in certain religions all their lives that they are wrong?

Comments:

Dr. G.D. James, born into a Hindu family and now a Christian minister with the Asia Evangelistic Fellowship, reminds us that "our response should be to treat these people of the cults as God treats them. God loves them. God wants them. God sympathizes with them. So let us not get angry with them. Let us not prejudice them because they are being misled. You don't get angry with a person (who is suffering from cancer) ... you feel sorry for him. So we are to love the people who are being misled ... so that they will be attracted to Christ" (Interview with Gary Randall, June 1982).

"Do not look upon him as an enemy, but warn him as a brother," (Col. 3:14).

Dilemma:

It seems almost too much to ask of me to completely reject all the beliefs that I trusted all these years. It is very hard to accept that I've been wrong!

Comment:

I know how incredibly painful it is to admit we've been deceived. Saying goodbye to cherished beliefs feels like saying goodbye to old friends. But some friends, like the one who robbed my apartment, are not really friends at all!

Dilemma:

But the seeker in New Age is not malicious or demon-possessed. All we want to do is to manifest the love of God.

Comment:

Another former Hindu, now a Christian, is Rabi Maharaj, who said in an interview on "Something Beautiful" in 1983 that he had attended a huge convention of New Agers in California. As he surveyed the masses of people promoting their wares and beliefs, he said he was aware of more satanic influence and demonic spirits there than in all his years in the Hindu position of a guru — and he wept. Often when he lectured in colleges, the scheduled lectures went into overtime, even past midnight, while young people kept challenging

Rabi about his new faith in Christ as opposed to the mystical viewpoints. Rabi said that at one point a young man said tearfully, "It may sound like we are (harassing) you with all our questions, but please ... it is just because we want to know the truth."

Dilemma:

It looks like a lot of Christians have lost interest in education and knowledge and all they do is read the Bible and little else.

Comment:

To be informed is to be equipped. Christianity is neither restricted to illiterates nor intellectuals. Noah Webster was quoted to have said, "All education without the Bible is useless."

Dilemma:

Just believing the Bible literally is hard for me to swallow. I've studied a lot of books that show how the Bible is full of errors, deletions and deeper meanings.

Comment:

"Who has understood the Mind (or Spirit) of the Lord, or instructed *Him* as His counselor?" (Isaiah 40:13). Apparently anyone who thinks he knows more than God.

"The teachings of these spirits would be so full of enlightenment, of deep truths, of superior knowledge and religious matter, plus worldly wisdom, that the unconscious victim would be gradually led on into darkness without noticing that he was being surrounded by false teaching and would be, to all practical intent, forgotten and superceded by something professing to be 'deeper.' Such is the method which we would expect the devil and his emissaries to use, and that is exactly what happens," (Raphael Gasson, *The Challenging Counterfeit,* Logos International, 1966-79).

Dilemma:

Come on, you really can't be a fundamentalist . . . If you take the Bible literally then you'd be looking for Jesus to appear as a household door, since he said "I am the Door!"

Comment:

Fundamentalism is defined in the dictionary as "a movement in the twentieth century Protestantism emphasizing the literal inerrancy of the Scriptures, the second coming of Jesus Christ, the virgin birth, physical resurrection and substitutionary atonement."

These admissions of the faith are not restricted to a few denominations, but they bind believers of the Christian church. If we say we take the Bible literally, it means that we take God at his word. We don't wear ourselves out trying to find deeper meanings or hidden messages, even though Paul wrote to Timothy, "No one would deny that this religion of ours is a tremendous mystery . . ." (I Tim. 3:4 Phillips Trans.). Also, in Colossians 2:4 ". . . that they may know the mystery of God, namely *Christ, in whom* are hidden *all* the treasures of wisdom and knowledge. I tell you this so that no one may deceive you with fine-sounding arguments."

Dilemma:

Isn't the Montessori method of teaching New Age in content and philosophy?

Comment:

We teachers used to say "for every person who operates a Montessori school, there is a different kind of school." Administrators promote their beliefs, and the Church Universal and Triumphant has its own Montessori International school. Perhaps the strength of the method (which relies on the didactic materials as the true teacher) is also its weakness. Children learn to trust their own progress and success as an inner authority. Christian Montessori schools have more freedom to teach the Bible as the authority. I still believe that the method is a good one for teaching independence and advancing academic skills.

Dilemma:

Don't some schools teach ideas about "invisible guides?"

Comment:

You are referring to confluent education, some of which does indeed promote this.

Editor Tom McMahon submitted an article to me written by Frances Adeney, entitled "Educators Look East." Ms. Adeney interviewed Dr. Beverly Galyean, promoter of this system in public schools and private ones, and reports that children are being taught through guided imagery to "visualize a light within them which contains all knowledge and all love, and to which they turn for insights and power." First graders are introduced to spirit guides although Galyean remarked that, "Of course we don't call them that in the public schools. We call them imaginary guides," (SCP Journal Winter 1981-82, Reprinted from Radix Magazine, Nov.–Dec. 1980).

I had never attended any conference workshops which

taught this formally, yet I practiced it for years during my teaching career. This is another example of how New Agers seem to know things without learning where the concepts originate. I had been deceived by my own spirit guides operating in meditative consciousness. Since then, I have repented for the doors that I opened to those little children and I pray that God will lead them to the true door, Jesus.

Dilemma:

I was active in some feminist meetings, and I am still in favor of their politics. What has that got to do with mysticism?

Comment:

There is a tendency to lure women into believing that they aren't just equal, but superior to men, especially spiritually.

Dave Hunt documents these teachings and explains that the "major force behind the women's movement was spiritual, not political, and is still gaining momentum. The Women's Movement is one of the most important parts of the New Age movement."

He refers to the title of one Women's Conference held in Southern California during April of 1982: "Women: The Leading Edge of the New Age." Its feminist therapist revealed that " 'the New Age will allow us to experience a sense of wholeness, a sense of connectedness with nature' (i.e. Mother Nature)." He mentions that "As any witch will proudly inform you, the oldest spirituality on earth is Wicca or witchcraft."

When I outlined the references to women's role in New Age to my friend who had been born into a coven, she confirmed this.

"Many of those involved in the Feminist Movement may sincerely believe it is a political crusade to gain equality with men. In fact, it is more than that: it is also a spiritual movement based partly upon a reawakening of 'goddess-consciousness,' and its real goal is matriarchy, not equality," Hunt said.

Dilemma:

Well, I spent too many years raising my consciousness to get stuck in the role of the obedient, subservient and mindless Christian wife. That "Total Woman" idea reminds me of the movie *The Stepford Wives* where the women are turned into robots that don't question their husbands' authority. All they do is discuss recipes and floor-wax!

Comment:

I hardly feel like a "Stepford Wife." When I divorced two men and tried to say it was because they weren't advanced enough spiritually, I now believe that had those relationships been founded in Christ and biblical standards none of us would have suffered in the ways we did. A Christian marriage is no guarantee against divorce, but the differences in relationships that invite regular prayer and scriptural priorities stand better odds against collapse, like one in eleven hundred instead of one out of two, as in non-Christian marriages. The "submissive wife" stereotype is far from reality among my married Christian sisters.

"When your husband loves you the way Christ loves the church, you know you're really *loved!*" Sally told me when her fiance' came to Jesus.

Gail likes to say, "You can tell how good a Christian a man is by how much joy his wife has!"

Red's favorite is, "If you want your wife to treat you like a king, treat her like a queen!"

Those affectionate descriptions may sound like mushy platitudes to a hardened militant feminist, but for women who have tried marriage without Jesus, it is an example of an endearment in sharing *agape love*.

Dilemma:

I'm mixed up about the whole issue of sexuality in New Age philosophies. Some say celibacy equates spirituality; some seem to prescribe the Kama Sutra for all kinds of activities; others promote group sex, sex therapy, bisexuality and homosexuality; still others claim that true mates exist on other planes. It's all very confusing.

Comment:

Of course! Philosophies based on Hindu doctrines (of many gods) are open to any number of non-biblical standards. But the Creator "is not the author of confusion," (I Cor. 14:33). His words provide godly guidelines as well as restrictions. It doesn't even gloss over man's failures; instead he offers forgiveness. Confusion leads to despair and despair too often to suicide. If Satan can lure you into a suicide pact with a "soul twin" he'll do anything to get you to believe his lies.

Dilemma:

What are your feelings about homosexuals now that you're a Christian?

Comment:

When I hear preachers quote all the scriptures condemning this practice, I recognize that they are correct — homosexuality is a sin. But I pray that Christians will at least have compassion for those trapped in this bondage. I've heard attitudes from three categories of homosexuals: those who blatantly flaunt their "gay pride" and have no intention of changing, others who insist that Jesus came to "take away our sins but not our sexuality" and attend churches that condone their preferences and Christians who have renounced the practice of homosexuality (as difficult as it was to do so) because as one man said it is a form of "idolatry and demonic possession."

One former lesbian, now a married Christian, pleaded with the church not to react to homosexuals as if it were the most horrendous and unforgivable sin in the world, but to remember *all sin is sin.* God hates sin but he loves sinners so much he sent his Son to die for them! This woman, with tears in her eyes, asked Christians to show love to homosexuals in order to bring them to repentance and forgiveness in Christ.

"It is because we were never treated with love," she said, "that we turned away from those who rejected us and looked for churches that don't preach repentance."

Dilemma:

I've heard the warnings about the individuals in New Age who are promoting dangerous doctrines. Why am I suspected of being in league with the devil just because I belong to a particular organization listed in the movement's directories? My beliefs aren't the same as the extremists involved!

Comment:

There is a notion among New Agers that one can pick and choose the philosophies that are more appealing and thus escape a world plan of delusion. A greater

percentage of participants in the movement are innocently involved in practices, causes and theories which
dove-tail by association.

*"Be ye not unequally yoked together with unbelievers:
for what fellowship hath righteousness with unrighteous-
ness? And what communion hath light with darkness?"*
(2 Cor. 6:14).

Repeatedly I have heard seekers insist that they are
not following the same goals as some New Age leaders
have outlined. Then I hear them talk about their zodiac
sign, or mind-over-matter or an assortment of related
beliefs. That's rather like saying you do not belong to a
secret club, yet you attend the meetings, use the code
words, align with the members and agree with most of
the tenets. You don't have to be a card-carrying member
to be recognized as a supporter.

Dilemma:

I don't see anything wrong with keeping decorative
statues or objects that Christians say I should get rid of.
That seems a bit extreme.

Comment:

It may seem so, but everyone I know who has gone
through a thorough housecleaning of occult objects and
paraphernalia has reported all kinds of beautiful results.
Once you have renounced those avenues and immersed
yourself in the fullness of Christ, you may begin to desire
items that glorify *him*. Besides, why advertise the enemy's
symbols? (See Acts 19:19).

I hardly think we should keep our children in isolation
bubbles. They are always fascinated by stories of outer
space and television programs are full of experiments
with psychic overtones. Rather, children can be informed

on what to look for as being "against God" and often the kids spot the clues before adults do.

Dilemma:

Isn't all this scrutiny over apostate doctrines rather like putting Christians under a microscope? We all have *some* differences of doctrinal opinions!

Comment:

Apostasy, or "falling away," a deliberate rejection of Jesus Christ's deity and redemption "differs therefore from error concerning truth, which may be as a result of ignorance (Acts 19:1-6), or heresy, which may be due to the snare of Satan (2 Tim. 2:25,26) both of which may consist with true faith ... Apostates depart from the faith, but not from the outward profession of Christianity (3:5)."

Born-again believers might be excused for being beguiled by erroneous concepts, but apostate teachers and church apostasy "is irremediable, and awaits judgment (2 Thess. 2:10-12; 2 Pet. 2:1-19; Jude 4, 8, 11-13, 16; Rev. 3:14-16)."

The theme of Colossians is described in the introduction of Paul's epistle in the Scofield Reference Bible: a "form of error was false mysticism, 'intruding into those things which he hath not seen' — the result of philosophic speculation. Because these are ever present perils, Colossians was written, not for that day only, but for the warning of the church in all days."

Paul warns in Galatians 1:6, "*I marvel that ye are so soon removed from him that called you into the grace of Christ unto another gospel: which is not another; but there be some that trouble you, and would pervert the gospel of Christ.*"

"Another gospel" is footnoted in Scofield as, "If the message excludes grace, or mingles law with grace as the means of either justification or sanctification or denies the fact or guilt of sin which alone gives grace its occasion and opportunity, it is 'another' gospel, and the preacher of it is under anathema of God."

Again, this other gospel, which is not another but "a perversion of the Gospel of the Grace of God," has one test — "it invariably denies the sufficiency of grace alone to save, keep and perfect, and mingles with grace some kind of human merit. In Galatia, it was law, in Colosse fanaticism," according to Scofield.

Dilemma:

I hardly think we have much to worry about that Nazism will rear again. It's the Communists we should keep our eye on.

Comment:

It would seem impossible that the world could ever allow such an inhumane event like the Holocaust to recur. But as the Baby Boom generation gets older, let us pray that our memory of that tragedy does not blur. The writer of the article "The Wangervogel," John De Graaf reminds us that "Hitler's talk of a mystical community ... won over large numbers of the young who had no memory of the horrors of World War I."

Leaders in the New Age Movement reveal that Communism makes them very nervous, yet little mention is made of Nazism. In a pamphlet by Summit Lighthouse entitled in part *Declaration of International Interdependence* columns of historical references are listed concerning atrocities perpetrated by Communists. Figures of lives lost are given, yet the only time the word Nazis appeared was within one sentence, "whereas, the Nazis were responsible for at least four-fifths of these losses, and the rest were the responsibility of the USSR ..." (Four-fifths is almost a whole pie according to my arithmetic). But bear in mind, Nazism is fascism and is rooted in the belief of Aryanism.

"In the book of Revelation the government of the Antichrist is to be headed by 'the beast that was dead and came back to life.' After extensive research, it is safe to say that the New Age Movement is identical in both belief systems and cosmology of the Nazism of Hitler — which I believe is the beast that was dead and came back to life" (Constance Cumbey, "Hidden Dangers of the Rainbow," page 73).

Communism has been thriving, whereas we have all assumed Nazism was squashed. But remember the youth of Germany. They had studied eastern mysticism and were later forming "Bible circles." Before their Aryan blond hair turned grey, they were goose-stepping into the Third Reich.

The historian Bruce L. Shelley warned us to take a lesson from the gnostics lest we attempt to "raise Christianity from the level of faith to a higher realm of intelligent knowledge ..." Aryanism pollutes Christianity in our time, too.

I received another item entitled *The True Teachings of Jesus Christ* by an anonymous sender. A cassette tape contained ninety minutes of scriptures, various references and name-calling which tried to prove that Jesus was a Gentile. The speaker accused all Jews and blacks of being "devils, created by Satan." Using the Bible and the precious name of Jesus Christ, the speaker continually attacked the nation of Israel and twisted prophecies to confirm his fears for "the white seed" of the "white

Adam!"

The tip-off that this poor man was in need of deliverance was that he claimed to be "the only man on the face of the earth who knows this." Whoever sent the tape may have hoped I would be in on the "secret conspiracy." However, it is merely more evidence that "the beast that was dead" is rearing its ugly head in the propaganda of Nazism.

Before we load our guns and suspect our neighbors of being Nazis or Communists, let us remember that our battle is not against each other but against spiritual forces in high places (See Eph. 6:12).

Dilemma:

What could be so wrong about allowing our spirits to leave our bodies? The Bible describes several incidents where great prophets of God were carried off in the spirit.

Comment:

If God Almighty invites you to glimpse heaven or travel to distant places, surely he will protect you as he leads. Such an experience should glorify God's purposes however, not merely satisfy your curiosity.

After I became a Christian I wanted to be certain if these O.O.B.E.s were of God. Five years later, during an unsavory dream, I experienced the familiar buzzing sound in my ears and felt my "soul body" drawing upwards. I briefly hoped that like the "great prophets" I too was about to "see heaven." Then I heard a voice. It was most certainly *not* my shepherd's voice, but that of the accuser, saying, "We have located the woman I told you about. We want her to *blend*."

In all my years on the Path, I never heard audible

voices and I used to feel "left out" since so many other Questers heard voices. This time, as I fought to resist the sensations of astral travel, my body felt frozen, my hands were drawn inward like an animal's claws and my teeth were clenched so tightly that I could barely cry out a muffled sound to my sleeping husband. I managed to grab his arm and communicate my terror, and Red lovingly held me and rebuked the enemy *"who accuses the brethren before God both day and night"* (See Rev. 12:9,10).

I believe that God allowed this experience to occur so close to the completion of my research because I had really wanted to soft-pedal some of the practices in New Age that I personally didn't think were so dangerous.

Dilemma:

There is a saying that "Prayer is talking to God, meditation is listening to God." Doesn't the Bible say we should meditate?

Comment:

Yes, upon God's Word. Look up Psalms 119:47-104 for the beautiful descriptions of the differences in meditation. Before I knew the Lord or his truth, I meditated privately and in groups. Constance Cumbey noted in her book that she observed meditations where the "participants are taken under progressively deeper levels of hypnosis and not brought back out!"

Dilemma:

I realized early on the Quest that hallucinogens and other mind-altering substances were not a permanent method for raising my consciousness but some of my experiences with drugs truly opened my eyes!

Comment:

The serpent said, *"For God doth know that in the day ye eat thereof, then your eyes shall be opened, and ye shall be as gods, knowing both good and evil"* (Gen. 3:5).

Whether you experimented with "eye-opening" drugs, mankind has been born under the curse of the original fall of man. Hence, our need to be born again.

It is not uncommon for drug-users to explain that while under the influence, "suddenly all bibles made sense," as Marilyn Ferguson reported in her book *The Aquarian Conspiracy*. However, Ms. Ferguson felt this to be a positive development, even if some "bibles" refute the story of Adam and Eve. Some attempt to convince the seeker that if he disregards the fact of man's fallen condition, then he is not in need of redemption.

Ms. Ferguson quoted Aldous Huxley to have praised the initial use of hallucinogens.

She says, "For many people in many cultures, psychedelic drugs have offered a beginning trail if seldom a fully transformative path. Huxley, who had no illusion about drugs as permanent routes to enlightenment, pointed out that even temporary self-transcendence would shake the entire society to its national roots," and that he "believed that the long-predicted religious revival in the United States would start with drugs, not evangelists," (*The Aquarian Conspiracy*, J.P. Tarcher, Inc., 1980, page 375).

Dilemma:

I gave up psychedelics years ago. But I don't see that there is much to worry about marijuana. After all, man made booze and chemicals, God made grass!

Comment:

It seems that of all the mind-altering substances, grass is the most difficult for many users to give up. Even new Christians struggle to justify this "mild and natural tranquilizer." Scientists have labored to understand this substance, and the side effects include memory-loss, lethargy and apathy. Alcohol, also abused, continues to cause *tragedies* in the lives of people who have become slaves to it.

Dilemma:

I suppose that if I don't repent and get saved you'll say I'm going to hell and burn forever. What kind of loving God would do such a thing to people who never even heard of Jesus Christ?

Comment:

What kind of a loving God would offer salvation only to those who managed to elevate their consciousness to enlightened perfection? I was brought up with the belief that neither heaven nor hell existed — they were only states of mind. Fire and brimstone sermons, scare-tactics and passing judgment will also be judged by God.

Ms. Cumbey renders Romans 2:1-6, for scriptural reference to Judgment Day and says "there may be many surprises for those 'Christians' who have deliberately apostasized or misled the body of Christ. They may see some poor pagan who did the best he could with the little knowledge he did possess standing redeemed and joyous before the throne while the apostates and hypocrites watch with gnashing of teeth from outside."

Dilemma:

In New Thought religion I have been taught to have a

positive self-image. There's so much emphasis in fundamental Christianity on everybody being such a miserable sinner. I don't feel like I'm such a bad person.

Comment:

The saying "a man who says he has no faults has just
added one more" might be considered. A positive mental attitude and self-esteem are desirable and healthy
stands, but gnostic doctrines end up over-emphasizing
self, and soon the ego is deified. (Remember Lucifer?)
Spiritual pride is the worst trap of any religion and
humility is honored by God. "He who exalts himself shall
be humbled; he who humbles himself shall be exalted"
(Matt. 23:12).

Everyone of us has fallen short of perfection. *"For
ALL have sinned and fall short of the glory of God"*
(Rom. 3:23).

Dilemma:

Well, I suppose Christians feel like the Bible tells
them to witness the gospel to everyone, but what gives
them the right to rearrange my life on a continuous
basis!

Comment:

None of us is so mature that we always behave correctly and surely we all have lapses of tact! The exhortation (or counsel, advice) that the Christian seeks to
offer, speaking truth in love, sometimes hurts. But we do
find times for "righteous indignation," and we are not
door-mats. *"Iron sharpens iron,"* (Prov. 27:17) and we
may ruffle each other's feathers occasionally.

"Their need to approach others as the lost while
(being) securely among the saved may be evidence of a

psychological condition to which the Christ seeks to come as corrector and healer, not encourager and condoner," Paul Clasper, (*Eastern Paths and the Christian Way*, Orbis Books, 1980, page 130).

Dilemma:

I know Christians who go to church every Sunday and then sin all week long.

Comment:

Sanctification toward holy living doesn't alway happen over-night! The difference is that where once an individual was unconcerned about "conscience" now he feels the tug of the Holy Spirit convicting him to press on to righteousness. (See 1 John 1:9).

14

From Initiation to Invitation

This book would not be complete unless I kept my promise to my dear friend Sally Obert, the one who most fervently prayed for my salvation while I was still unaware of the dangers I was courting during my Quest. Sally remarked that "there are lots of books that tell you that you need to *be* saved, but not many that tell you *how* to be sure you're saved." I agree.

The New Ager yearns to be a worthy initiate of higher consciousness so he joins private study groups, signs up for courses, attends lectures and tries to meditate with determination and discipline. Advancement comes by degrees or steps and each is viewed seriously.

Being born again of the Spirit of God also has steps. But it doesn't take days, weeks, months, years or life-times. It can take only minutes and is offered for eternity! Rather than initiation it is an invitation so no one will force you. It is said that "Jesus is a gentleman; he waits outside the door and knocks, longing for you to open your heart and bid him to come in."

Inviting Jesus Christ as your Saviour, your Lord and Master is so simple that when very little children accept him and grow into adults they tell of the day they gave their hearts to the Lord. In fact, we are to become just like a little child if we want to enter into God's kingdom — humble, trusting and sincere. The prayer often called "the sinner's prayer" is the prayer of salvation and in similar form anyone who has repeated this prayer and meant it in his or her heart is assured of forgiveness and grace — and you will know it!

Intellect will have to step aside for a moment. Emotionalism is not required although most people are moved to tears as they humble themselves before God. For example, God has restored all those years when I hid my tears from the sight of others; I weep openly so often when I worship God that my my husband gave me a collection of dainty handkerchiefs.

Fantastic sensations don't have to accompany your moment of salvation, either. In fact, you may not feel anything right away but remember, this is a conscious decision of commitment to God that you are making and by deciding to believe upon Jesus Christ you are accepting what Jesus already did for mankind and for you as an individual.

Are you ready now to prayerfully prepare your heart to receive him? It is the single most important decision of your life: where you will spend eternity!

Those of us who have had heavy occultic backgrounds or who have had relatives involved in witchcraft must seriously list the practices and renounce all of them and pray for deliverance from generational bondage as well as from our own participation. Other born-again believers may minister this deliverance for you but if you have no one "plead the blood of Jesus Christ" over all of these sins and ask God to forgive you.

If you notice any peculiar tendency to feel tired, a bit nauseated, fearful or distracted right now, please know that it is not God who is hindering you but the adversary. Don't worry, he is already a defeated foe and he knows he has lost another victory. Right now "heaven holds its breath" as you try to decide which direction you will take. Jesus tells us in Luke 15:7, "There will be more joy in heaven over one sinner that repents than over ninety-nine who need no repentance."

This is your day and one you will never forget. Find a quiet place and humble your heart and say the words aloud in the presence of God.

PRAYER OF SALVATION

1. Recognize that you have fallen short of perfection and have attempted to know God selfishly.

"God, I know I have sinned."

2. Repent of your sins. Repentance is "turning in another direction," experiencing godly grief about your condition of rebellion.

"God, I'm sorry for my sins. I commit myself to your ways and renounce my involvement in the ways you have forbidden in your Word."

3. Forgiveness from God is a gift, unearned, undeserved, but you need to ask the Father for this gift.

"Father, please forgive me."

4. Decide to believe that Jesus is God's Son, that he gave his life so you could know redemption, that he rose again and ascended to the Father.

"Jesus, you are God's Son; I know that you died on the

cross for me; that you rose on the third day and ascended to the Father."

5. Invite Jesus into your heart to be your Saviour, your Lord, your master.

"Jesus, I ask you to come into my heart and reign there forever."

6. Thank Him!

"Jesus, I thank you for coming into my heart and saving me from my sins. I know that I am forgiven and that you have given me eternal life in your kingdom."

7. Tell somebody you have made a commitment to Christ Jesus.

"For it is with your heart that you believe and are justified, and it is with your mouth that you confess and are saved," (Rom. 10:10).

Did you say "I do" to the bridegroom? If you prayed this prayer in your heart, Happy Birthday! You have become born again into the family of God! Your old self is being crucified and you have become a new creation! If you are Jewish by heritage, you remain a Jew, but, as Messianic Jews sometimes say of themselves, a "completed Jew." May you grow in grace and follow him all the days of your life!

Now you will need to keep a commandment to be baptized, (Mark 16:16). There are differing views about the method; some say sprinkling, some say total immersion. You may think it isn't necessary to be baptized, especially if you had been christened at infancy, but this is an adult decision you are making whether you are eight or eighty! Remember, Jesus didn't need to be baptized for he had no sin, but he requested John to baptize him publicly to set an example and to fulfill the law.

Even though I had a private ceremony, I did go for a

formal baptism with my husband later when our pastor performed the ceremony for us in a church member's pool. I sure didn't want to skip anything.

Find a church where you can have fellowship with other believers. The Word says, "Let us not give up meeting together, as some are in the habit of doing, but let us encourage one another — and all the more as you see the Day approaching" (Heb. 10:25). Denomination is not the issue, but be sure the church teaches the Bible and worships the Trinity. It may take some shopping until you find a church that is alive.

Read the Bible through. Get familiar with both Testaments. Study it, underline it, memorize passages. And New Age bibles don't count. There are several standard Bibles with references and you may begin to collect quite a few versions.

A Scofield Reference Bible (the one my husband inherited from his mother) renders a passage by Jesus with which I would like to close. It is taken from Matthew 11:28, 29 and is noted as "The new message of Jesus." The Master who gave us a "New Covenant" with his precious blood is all the "new" any of us need.

"Come unto me, all ye that labour and are heavy laden, and I will give you rest. Take my yoke upon you, and learn of me; for I am meek and lowly in heart: and ye shall find rest unto your souls."

Lord Jesus, thank you for rest from the quest. I know I shall never thirst again. I'm ready for the rest of you, for the rest of my life!

EPILOGUE

I've been a New Ager most of my life but I will be a Christian for the rest of my life. How about you? If you have found rest from the Quest in Jesus Christ, Messiah and Lord of Lords, rejoice! I would enjoy hearing from you. We have the assurance that when we are born again unto Christ, we are family; and one day we will meet in Paradise! Till then . . .

Elissa Lindsey McClain
P.O. Box 155
Longwood, Florida 32750

RECOMMENDED READING LIST

In addition to books mentioned and quoted from in this testimony, the following books are highly informative.

Death of a Guru: A Hindu Comes to Christ
by R. Maharaj, Publ. A.J. Holman, 1979

Great Expectations:
America and the Baby Boom Generation
by Landon Y. Jones, 1980 Publ. The Putnam Group (Coward, McCann, Geoghegan)

True and False Prophets
by Don Basham, Manna Books, 1973

The Most Dangerous Game
by Don Basham, Dick Leggatt, Manna Books, 1974

The Riddle of Reincarnation
by Walter Martin, Vision House Publishers

Reincarnation, Edgar Cayce & the Bible
by Phillip J. Swihart, InterVarsity Press, 1975

Reincarnation and Christianity
by Robert Morey, Publ. by Bethany Fellowship, Inc. 1980

Earth's Earliest Ages
by G.H. Pember, Kregel Publications (first edition 1942; rev. 1979)

MORE FAITH-BUILDING BOOKS FROM HUNTINGTON HOUSE

The Agony of Deception, by Ron Rigsbee. This is the story of a young man who through surgery became a woman and now, through the grace of God, is a man again. Share this heartwarming story of a young man as he struggles through the deception of an altered lifestyle only to find hope and deliverance in the Grace of God.

America Betrayed, by Marlin Maddoux. This book presents stunning facts on how the people of the United States have been brainwashed. This hard-hitting new book exposes the forces in our country which seek to destroy the family, the schools and our values. Maddoux is a well-known radio journalist and host of "Point of View."

Backward Masking Unmasked, by Jacob Aranza. Are Rock and Roll stars using the technique of backward masking to implant their own religious and moral values into the minds of young people? Are these messages satanic, drug-related and filled with sexual immorality? Jacob Aranza answers these and other questions.

Backward Masking Unmasked Tape, by Jacob Aranza. Hear actual Satanic Messages and judge for yourself.

Close Calls, by Don Garlits. Many times "Big Daddy" Don Garlits has escaped death — both on and off the drag racing track. This is the story of drag racing's most famous and popular driver in history. Share his trials and triumphs and the Miracle of God's Grace in his heart.

The Divine Connection, by Dr. Donald Whitaker. This

is a Christian Guide to Life Extension. It specifies biblical principles for how to feel better and live longer.

Globalism: America's Demise, by William Bowen, Jr. A national bestseller, this book warns us about the globalists — some of the most powerful people on earth — and their plans to totally eliminate God, the family and the United States as we know it today. Globalism is the vehicle the humanists are using to implement their secular humanistic philosophy to bring about their one-world government.

God's Timetable for the 1980's, by Dr. David Webber. This book presents the end-time scenario as revealed in God's Word and carefully explained by Dr. Webber, the Radio Pastor of the highly acclaimed Southwest Radio Church. This timely book deals with a wide spectrum of subjects including the dangers of the New Age Movement, end-time weather changes, robots and biocomputers in prophecy.

The Hidden Dangers of the Rainbow, by Constance Cumbey. This #1 National Bestseller was the first book to fully expose the New Age Movement. The Movement's goal is to set up a one-world order under the leadership of a false messiah.

The Hidden Dangers of the Rainbow Tape, by Constance Cumbey. Mrs. Cumbey, a trial lawyer from Detroit, Michigan, gives inside information on the New Age Movement in this teaching tape.

Murdered Heiress ... Living Witness, by Dr. Petti Wagner. This is the story of Dr. Petti Wagner — heiress to a large fortune — who was kidnapped and murdered for her wealth, yet through a miracle of God lives today.

A Reasonable Reason to Wait, by Jacob Aranza. God speaks specifically about premarital sex, according to Aranza. The Bible also provides a healing message for those who have already been sexually involved before marriage.

Rest From the Quest, by Elissa Lindsey McClain. This is the candid account of a former New Ager who spent the first 29 years of her life in the New Age Movement, the occult and Eastern Mysticism. This is an incredible inside look at what really goes on in the New Age Movement.

The Twisted Cross, by Joseph Carr. One of the most important works of our decade, **The Twisted Cross** clearly documents the occult and demonic influence on Adolph Hitler and the Third Reich which led to the holocaust killing of more than six million Jews.

Yes, send me the following books:

_____ copy (copies) of **The Agony Of Deception** @ $6.95   = _____

_____ copy (copies) of **America Betrayed** @ $5.95   = _____

_____ copy (copies) of **Backward Masking Unmasked** @ $4.95   = _____

_____ copy (copies) of **Backward Masking Unmasked Cassette Tape** @ $5.95   = _____

_____ copy (copies) of **Close Calls** @ $6.95   = _____

_____ copy (copies) of **The Divine Connection** @ $4.95   = _____

_____ copy (copies) of **Globalism: America's Demise** @ $6.95   = _____

_____ copy (copies) of **God's Timetable For The 1980's** @ $5.95   = _____

_____ copy (copies) of **The Hidden Dangers Of The Rainbow** @ $5.95   = _____

_____ copy (copies) of **Murdered Heiress Living Witness** @ $5.95   = _____

_____ copy (copies) of **A Reasonable Reason To Wait** @ $4.95   = _____

_____ copy (copies) of **Rest From The Quest** @ $5.95   = _____

_____ copy (copies) of **Take Him To The Streets** @ $5.95   = _____

_____ copy (copies) of **The Twisted Cross** @ $7.95   = _____

_____ copy (copies) of **Who Will Rise UP** @ $5.95   = _____

At bookstores everywhere or order direct from: Huntington House, Inc., P.O. Box 53788, Lafayette, LA 70505.

Send check/money order or for faster service VISA/Mastercard orders call toll-free 1-800-572-8213. Add: Freight and handling, $1.00 for the first book ordered, 50¢ for each additional book.

Enclosed is $ _____ including Postage.

Name _____

Address _____

City _____ State and Zip _____